P9-CQS-712

Skary Childrin

-AND THE CAROUSEL OF SORROW-

BY

KATY TOWELL

Alfred A. Knopf

New York

THIS IS A BORZOI BOOK PUBLISHED BY ALFRED A. KNOPF

This is a work of fiction. Names, characters, places, and incidents either are the product of the author's imagination or are used fictitiously. Any resemblance to actual persons, living or dead, events, or locales is entirely coincidental.

Copyright © 2011 by Katy Towell

All rights reserved. Published in the United States by Alfred A. Knopf, an imprint of Random House Children's Books, a division of Random House, Inc., New York. Originally published in hardcover in the United States by Alfred A. Knopf, an imprint of Random House Children's Books, in 2011.

Knopf, Borzoi Books, and the colophon are registered trademarks of Random House, Inc.

Visit us on the Web! randomhouse.com/kids

Educators and librarians, for a variety of teaching tools, visit us at RHTeachersLibrarians.com

The Library of Congress has cataloged the hardcover edition of this work as follows:
Towell, Katy.
Skary childrin and the carousel of sorrow / by Katy Towell. — 1st ed.
p. cm.
Summary: In Widowsbury, an isolated village where people believe "known is good, new is bad," three outcasts from the girls' school join forces with a home-schooled boy to uncover and combat the evil that is making people disappear.
ISBN 978-0-375-86859-7 (trade) — ISBN 978-0-375-96860-0 (lib. bdg.) — ISBN 978-0-375-89931-7 (ebook)
[1. Supernatural—Fiction. 2. Schools—Fiction. 3. Ghosts—Fiction. 4. Merry-go-round—Fiction.] I. Title.
II. Title: Scary children and the carousel of sorrow. III. Title: Carousel of sorrow.
PZ7.T6488Skc 2011 [Fic]—dc22 2010038830

ISBN 978-0-375-87240-2 (tr. pbk.)

Printed in the United States of America

March 2013

10 9 8 7 6 5 4 3 2 1

First Trade Paperback Edition

Random House Children's Books supports the First Amendment and celebrates the right to read.

For my parents, Gina and Tony

Contents

CHAPTER ONE

New-Librarian Day

There was once, in the Pernicious Valley, a strange little town by the name of Widowsbury. It wasn't marked on any map. No roads led in or out of it. Only by train could one reach this forgotten place, but few who knew of it ever dared. The engineers spoke of ghosts in the hills, and they called these hills the Devil's Thimbles.

Just outside the Thimbles, at the point where the highway ended, was a sign that a vandal had altered to read IF YOU LIVED HERE YOU'D REGRET IT BY NOW. No one ever bothered to fix it. There wasn't much point, and anyway, it was true. Widowsbury was dreadfully cursed.

But even the most dreadfully cursed places were not always so.

There was a time when Widowsbury was the Plum Pie Capital of the World. The skies were still blue in those days. Colorful gardens decorated each storybook house. Laughter and music drifted from the square. City folk would come for the famous springtime parades and say, "What a delightful little town. Perhaps I'll retire here one

1

day." But that was before the roads were sealed off. Before everything went wrong.

They say it was a storm that ruined Widowsbury. Some say it wasn't a storm at all but evil's kettle boiling over. And when it ripped through the town for twelve straight days, it tore open a gate through which escaped all sorts of foul, rotten things. There *were* such things as vampires. There *were* such things as ghosts. There were *absolutely* such things as mad scientists who reanimated the dead. The once-perfect little haven became a beacon for everything bad in the world. Nothing and nobody unfamiliar would ever be trusted again, for one could never be sure what secrets waited under the surface.

There was peace again for a few years after the Storm. And then, one gray December morning twelve years to the day, a most troublesome stranger came to town.

Adelaide Foss slouched at the breakfast table, her cheek resting in one hand as her other hand poked at the eggs on her toast with fingernails that were just a bit too long. In fact, Adelaide's nails were alarmingly pointy, much like her ears, which she kept hidden behind twin black braids. At the front of the dining hall, the headmistress, Mrs. Merryweather, gave the Breakfast Lecture. It was an ordinary day at Madame Gertrude's School for Girls. Which, for awkward Adelaide, meant it would probably be a bad one.

"Posture is of the utmost importance in the civilized world," Mrs. Merryweather droned. "For a true lady must be recognized as such before she even utters a word!"

Adelaide heard the sound of fabric as someone slid across the bench to her. Without even looking, she knew it was Becky Buschard. One of the older girls.

"What's the matter with your eggs?" Becky whispered. "Not bloody enough for you?"

There was a smattering of muffled giggles as Becky slid back to her friends.

"Ah-ooooooooh!" one of them softly howled. Adelaide pretended not to hear, though it hardly did any good. In truth, she possessed a freakish ability to hear absolutely everything, sometimes even a mile away.

"A woman without balance in her step is a woman without balance in her life," Mrs. Merryweather lectured. With her hooked nose and her long black gown, she looked like one of Widowsbury's crows. Adelaide often wondered how she blinked at all with her silver hair pulled back in such a tight knot.

Adelaide stared off to the right, doing her best to ignore the faces made at her from the left. At the end of her table sat Maggie Borland, with two feet of empty space between her and the others. Nobody ever sat close to Maggie. Her wild brown hair made her look like Medusa, and her jumper was always stained. At the moment, she seemed wholly absorbed in her toast, which she carved into smaller and smaller pieces for no apparent reason. Every once in a while, she stabbed an egg, pounding the tines of her fork into a useless sculpture with each blow. Adelaide was fascinated. But then Maggie glanced up, and Adelaide hurriedly looked away.

There were rumors that Maggie had tossed a teacher through

a window at her old school, and that the teacher only survived by catching on to the sill. Adelaide didn't know if it was true, but she kept a safe distance all the same. This proved difficult, as Maggie was always in detention whenever she was, and Adelaide was in detention every day.

"When greeting new acquaintances, a lady must be reserved with her initial affection," Mrs. Merryweather went on.

Adelaide turned her attention to the other girl she saw in detention on a daily basis: Beatrice Alfred. Beatrice, simply put, was weird. She looked like a porcelain doll come to life—pale and tiny, with unnaturally dark eyes and short black hair topped with an oversized bow. She was in the Nines class, but she was only seven. Adelaide wondered if this explained Beatrice's peculiarities. Weren't really smart people supposed to be kind of odd?

Even now, Beatrice appeared to be whispering to something in her front pocket. *Who does she think she's talking to?* thought Adelaide with a shiver.

"Which brings me to my announcement," the headmistress continued. "Today we are expecting the arrival . . ."

Adelaide's breath caught in her throat.

". . . of a new . . ."

Please don't say what I think you're going to say! she prayed.

". . . librarian," Mrs. Merryweather concluded.

"Oh no," Adelaide groaned aloud.

"She is not from Widowsbury," Mrs. Merryweather explained, "but I assure you she has many references, and she is quite safe. She will, I hope, be joining us shortly, and I would like for you all to be on your very best behavior!"

Adelaide's palms began to sweat. This, under no uncertain terms, was Very Bad News.

"But there is one more thing!" said Mrs. Merryweather.

Her eyes narrowed. Her jaw clenched. She raised a long, bony finger and pointed.

Here it comes, thought Adelaide.

"You!" Mrs. Merryweather hissed at her.

She did the same to Maggie and Beatrice.

"You three are to be isolated from the others! You will be separated from the other students. You will be separated from each other. I will not give you any opportunity to frighten away *this* librarian before she even begins!"

Adelaide heard snickering behind her and felt her face grow hot.

"Don't think I've forgotten for an instant what you did to the others," said Mrs. Merryweather as she moved between the tables. "The incident with the chair . . ."

She glared at a scowling Maggie.

"The little present you left for Mrs. Elise."

She paused at a cowering Beatrice.

"Your campaign of terror against Mrs. Elizabeth!"

She watched Adelaide for a long time. Adelaide reddened. *I was only trying to warn her! I'm not the one who put the spiders in her bed! Not that she didn't deserve it,* she thought but could not say.

"No, I haven't forgotten," snarled Mrs. Merryweather, "and for that reason, I will make an example of each of you! I will show our new arrival that you can and will be controlled!"

Some of the other girls began to laugh.

"Quiet, ladies!" snapped Mrs. Merryweather. "Do not reward these children with your attention. For that is what they are. What they will always be. Rude. Spiteful. Wicked. Children. Their unwillingness to adhere to the vision of the great Madame Gertrude—may she rest peacefully—well, I dare say it scares me."

Yes, but you scare everybody, thought Adelaide.

"Miss Alfred!" said Mrs. Merryweather. "I want you to move to the small table at the far right corner. Miss Borland! To the table in the far left corner. And *you,* Miss Foss. To the table in the front center!"

The dining hall erupted with the cackles of three hundred schoolgirls, and this time, Mrs. Merryweather made no attempt to silence them.

"Scary childrennnnnn!" sang Becky as Adelaide marched to her seat in humiliation.

Yes, it was going to be a rotten day. New-Librarian Day always was. Librarians were supposed to read a lot and help you find the books you wanted. But all they ever did for Adelaide was force her to write punishment sentences until her hands turned red. Or yell at her for sneezing. Or make her sit as still and quiet as she possibly could with nothing to distract her from all the little sounds of the old building filling her head like a hundred symphonies playing different tunes at once. For Adelaide, librarians were torturers, and each new one was worse than the last.

Directly across the street was a squarish tower of red bricks that housed Rudyard School for Boys, the town's only other school since Widowsbury School had fallen victim to a sinkhole for the sixth time. Outside it stood Steffen Weller, the son of the Rudyard School cook. Today was his ninth birthday, and he was spending it by himself, doodling on the many flyers that were tacked to the wall. KNOW YOUR SURROUNDINGS! REPORT ANYTHING DIFFERENT TO THE COUNCIL AT ONCE! they said. He saw these flyers everywhere, and it seemed like fresh ones were being pasted over the old ones every day. They usually included Mayor Templeton's official seal beside a photo of the mayor looking very stern. Steffen drew glasses on him and grinned, pleased with his work.

Then he heard a sound like someone dragging their feet. Or perhaps a body. *Zombies!* he thought with a thrill. He had always wanted to meet a zombie. But it was only a woman coming up the road, her boots caked in mud. She carried a large black leather suitcase upon which she had pasted pictures of flowers. It looked as if it weighed more than she did.

Steffen had never seen her before.

Most Widowsburians feared newcomers, but Steffen never understood this. New people were exciting! Not quite as exciting as zombies, but Steffen's father said those had all been "dealt with" a long time ago. He supposed he'd never see one now.

"Hello," said Steffen, but the clearly exhausted woman did not appear to hear him.

He watched her for a while as she trudged wearily toward the enormous white cathedral of the girls' school. Then he shrugged and went back to drawing on flyers. REMEMBER THE STORM! said this one. KNOWN IS GOOD. NEW IS BAD!

He was drawing a mustache on it when he heard another commotion coming from the opposite end of the road. Steffen turned around and saw a man in a straw hat and a pink-and-white-striped apron approaching, dragging behind him a large wooden cart. The man looked young. Certainly older than any of the Rudyard boys, but definitely younger than Steffen's father. His cart was full of crates, jars, various tools, stakes, and something that looked like an oversized clock.

"Are you new in town, too?" Steffen asked the man. He hadn't meant to be rude, but two newcomers in one day! It was unheard of.

The man stopped and held up his hands. "I don't want any trouble!" he explained. It sounded as if he'd already gotten his share of it.

"Then what are you doing in Widowsbury?" asked Steffen.

"It . . . seemed like as good a place as any?" said the man uncertainly.

Steffen, remembering his manners, walked over and extended a mittened hand.

"Sorry. I'm Steffen Weller," he said. "What's your name?"

The man smiled and shook Steffen's hand with both of his.

"Zoethout's the name! Lyle Zoethout! Purveyor of sweets, treats, and delicious delights!" he said cheerfully. "And gosh, I'm glad to hear a friendly voice. Yours is the first I've heard since I got in on the midnight train!"

Steffen gaped. "The Midnight? Really?" he gasped, for the

midnight train was a thing of legend in Widowsbury. It first passed through about six years ago and had done so every night since. No one ever saw the train, but anyone awake at that hour could hear its clanging and its chugging and that lost, lonely whistle. His dad said it was all nonsense, of course, and that people would see it if they only went outside, but tales of the Midnight still held Steffen's imagination fast.

Lyle Zoethout didn't appear to know about those tales. He just blinked in confusion and then got right to his point. "Say, I'm setting up my stand today," he said, "and I sure could use an extra pair of hands. Do you know anyone who'd be willing to help? I can't pay except in candy right now, but it's the best candy there is, and that's my guarantee."

Steffen thought for a moment. The only person he could possibly ask would be his own father. But as skeptical as the senior Weller was about Widowsbury's superstitions, even he didn't care for new folk. He probably wouldn't like Steffen hanging around one, either, but he was busy with the day's lunch preparations, and that was never a good time to bother him.

"I guess I've got some time," said Steffen. He was relieved when Mr. Zoethout didn't laugh at him. Instead, the latter asked, "How are you with a hammer?"

"I was practically born holding a hammer!" Steffen said proudly.

"Fantastic!" Mr. Zoethout exclaimed. "Pleased to make your acquaintance, by the way. You can just call me Mr. Z. What sort of candy do you like, Mr. Weller?"

"Oh. Um," Steffen began, fidgeting with his jacket buttons. "I don't really like candy that much. It makes my stomach hurt. I'd much rather have peanut butter any old day, but that's okay. You don't have to pay me anything."

Mr. Zoethout gawked at Steffen.

"You don't like candy?"

"I—I'm sorry," Steffen stuttered. "I'm sure it's very good!"

"What kind of kid doesn't like candy?" Mr. Zoethout murmured to himself. Then he shrugged and chuckled.

"Never mind about that," he said. "I'm just glad to have your help. Say, maybe I'll come up with a new line of peanut butter treats! I'll call them Steffens."

Steffen laughed. He liked this newcomer, and it didn't matter if he got paid for his work or not. He was just pleased as punch to be of use to someone other than his father for once.

Adelaide sat stiff as a board at her new seat. By now, the mockery of her schoolmates had long been replaced with the sound of their conversations. She glanced over at Beatrice, who was now petting some invisible something in her hand. On the other side of the room, Maggie tipped back in her chair, scowling more than ever, looking exactly like someone who'd throw a person through a window. *I'm not like them*, thought Adelaide. *I'm normal. They're the scary ones!*

Beatrice looked over at her and offered a tiny wave, but Adelaide ignored it. She had enough trouble on her own. If anyone thought she was friends with the other two, all hope of relief from the constant ridicule would be lost.

Then she heard it. The doorbell. Nobody else seemed to notice it, but new librarians didn't mean to her schoolmates what they meant to her. She saw a maid scurry over to Mrs. Merryweather, who nodded and rushed out of the room.

Adelaide strained to hear, pushing back the curtain of sounds created by her schoolmates as they crunched their toast and talked and talked and talked. If she concentrated, she could hear the staccato clip of Mrs. Merryweather's steps as she rushed from the dining hall to the main hall with its tall pillars and portraits of dead people. She heard the maid's hurried breathing as she raced ahead to the foyer to open the heavy doors. She heard Mrs. Merryweather's taffeta skirts brush past the pedestal that held a bust of Madame Gertrude. And then . . .

"Miss Peet? Miss Delia Peet?" she heard Mrs. Merryweather ask.

"Please! Call me Delia," said a younger woman.

At least she's not old and creepy, Adelaide noted. But then it was often the younger ones who were the meanest.

"That sort of familiarity is for the students, Miss Peet. I am Miriam Merryweather. And you are very late!" snapped the headmistress.

"Oh. I—I'm sorry," said the younger woman. "I'm afraid the driver never arrived, and I couldn't get anyone else to stop for me! Perhaps your driver misunderstood? Is there another station?"

"The driver never . . . !" Mrs. Merryweather exclaimed. "Oh

dear. I shall have a word with Elmer Whitley when I see him next. Do come in. The girls are nearly through with their breakfast, which leaves me very little time to orient you!"

Adelaide took a few deep breaths and told herself that she had been through this before and could handle it again. But the pounding in her chest only worsened when Mrs. Merryweather returned to the dining hall with her guest following closely. The new librarian was petite, pretty, and neatly dressed in a brown wool coat and little round glasses. Her auburn hair was pinned back in a bun and decorated with a single monarch-butterfly pin. She had a kind look to her face, but Adelaide had long learned that librarians, like books, could not be judged by their covers.

"Ladies!" Mrs. Merryweather announced. "I would like you all to meet your new librarian. You may call her Miss Delia."

Adelaide froze. Maggie rolled her eyes. Beatrice tucked her invisible pet safely in her pocket. The other students turned in unison, a sea of gray cotton jumpers and white blouses.

"Good morning, Miss Delia," they greeted in wary, scattered mumbles.

Miss Delia waved to them, and with a nose as sensitive as her ears, Adelaide caught a whiff of orange-scented hand cream.

"Thank you, ladies. You may finish your breakfast," said Mrs. Merryweather. She turned to Miss Delia and went on to talk of the endless achievements of other students.

"That is Maria Flores. She earned perfect marks in penmanship last year. I expect she'll have an excellent future in dictation! That's

Becky Buschard. She's the pride and joy of our school, Miss Peet, and just yesterday she won the lead part in our annual play! Now, Christine Park—"

"Excuse me, Mrs. Merryweather," Miss Delia interrupted.

No, no, no. Don't look at me. I'm not here, Adelaide silently pleaded. But it was too late. The new librarian was staring right at her.

"What about those three?"

"Pardon?" Mrs. Merryweather said.

"The three girls seated away from the others. I couldn't help noticing that they don't look well. I know of a lovely tea that would put the color back in their cheeks if . . . it's a . . . cold . . ."

Miss Delia's voice trailed off.

Mrs. Merryweather's lips tightened. "They're well enough," she muttered. "Miss Peet, I should tell you now that any attempt to impress me beyond hard work will fall flat in this school."

"Oh, I didn't mean—!"

"But it was good of you to point them out, as you will need the advance warning." Here the headmistress lowered her voice, though Adelaide could hear her all the same. She almost wished she couldn't.

"Those three, Miss Peet, are my Trio of Trouble," said Mrs. Merryweather. "This is why I have seated them away from their peers. They are a constant source of grief for me, and no wonder! Their families all arrived in Widowsbury after the Big Storm."

"The Big Storm?" asked Miss Delia.

"Yes!" snapped Mrs. Merryweather without explanation. "The

one with the untamed curls is Maggie Borland. She's twelve, and a more slovenly, ill-tempered child you will never meet! Her parents ran off to join a circus or some nonsense. At least we're rid of them for the semester. The little one on the other side—that's Beatrice Alfred. Comes from a family of 'celebrity morticians.' Embalmers to the Stars, they call themselves. Good heavens! What a relief it was when they took to traveling for their work, though it is far too late for their influence to be reversed. Beatrice is an exceedingly bright child. In fact, she is two years ahead of the other girls her age! But she has filled her head with such morbid fascinations that there is little room for more. Her spelling! Mercy, her spelling! We have tried to correct her, but I fear she is simply too disturbed."

"Disturbed?" asked Miss Delia. "How do you mean?"

"She has a preoccupation with dead animals, Miss Peet, and she has been known to keep them as pets," said Mrs. Merryweather with a grimace. "She says their spirits are her friends!"

Miss Delia put her hand to her heart. "How very sad! But it's sweet in a way, don't you think? What about the one with the braids? My, what big eyes she has!"

Adelaide quickly pretended to examine something on her plate.

"That," Mrs. Merryweather said with disgust, "is Adelaide Foss. She's eleven. Wretched girl, it must be said. I have serious concerns about her ability to conform, Miss Peet! Serious concerns!"

Mrs. Merryweather leaned closer to the young librarian.

"She claims she hears things. Things nobody else ever hears.

And did you know there are some who say her parents are werewolves? Oh, they *claim* they are doctors researching medicine abroad, but it sounds highly suspicious to me!"

"Werewolves!" Miss Delia laughed. "Forgive me, but I don't think I believe that."

"I would doubt it, too, had I not seen all that I've seen over the years. Now I think I would believe almost anything," said Mrs. Merryweather. "Nevertheless, you will have to become more acquainted with those girls than you'll care to. Until they learn to behave like the others, they will spend every single recess of their school career in detention!"

"Goodness me!" said Miss Delia.

"And detention," Mrs. Merryweather added with a dramatic pause, "is always in the library!"

Adelaide's blood went cold at the mention of that terrible place. *Please let this librarian be nice,* she wished. *Please, please, please let her understand!*

"Yes, they are a trying group," Mrs. Merryweather was saying to Miss Delia. "Therefore, anything you feel must be done to maintain discipline you have my permission to try. Anything!"

She led the new librarian from the dining hall, talking of boring things like rules and wages and where the washrooms were. Adelaide stopped listening. It hardly mattered what they said now. The prospect of renewed library time was enough to ruin her entire morning. More than her mornings were usually ruined! Even so, she was determined more than ever to avoid winding up in detention yet again. There had to be a way.

I am not a scary child, she reminded herself. *I'm completely normal and no matter what, I will only do normal things today.*

She repeated this to herself throughout the morning, desperately hoping that if she could just avoid notice, she might escape the misfortune that followed her most other days despite her best efforts. By lunchtime, she began to think she had succeeded, for recess would be next and no one had yet mentioned detention. Perhaps this Miss Delia was still becoming acquainted, and there would be no library time today. Or maybe Adelaide would be assigned a few janitorial tasks, just as she had been since the last librarian's hasty retreat.

She was thinking of all this while searching for a seat in the dining hall when a sudden impact to her left side sent her lunch tray flying. Mashed potatoes somersaulted through the air. Peas scattered about the floor like marbles. The dining hall fell so quiet one could have heard a pin drop or, in this case, the sticky *plop* of Salisbury steak as it slid from the front of Adelaide's jumper to the marble floor.

Before her stood none other than Becky Buschard, a smirk of satisfaction creeping across her lips.

"I'm sorry, I didn't recognize you without fur all over your face," said Becky in her nasal voice. Her blond ponytail bobbed like a snake hanging from a tall, skinny tree.

The other students went back to their lunches. To them, it was just another day.

"I am *not* a werewolf," said Adelaide.

Becky cupped a hand to her ear and bent down.

"Excuse me?" she asked. "Could you say that in English, please? I don't speak *dog*."

"I'm not a dog!" Adelaide insisted, her fists clenched.

But Becky was already laughing and walking away.

"Did you see how red she was?" she snickered to one of her friends.

Adelaide was about to storm after her when suddenly, out of nowhere, *something* came soaring through the air at impossible speed. All eyes turned to the brown blur, mouths forming an *Ohhhh!* as it streaked toward its target, striking Becky's head with a delicious smack. *It* was a Salisbury steak, the force of which was so great it knocked Becky right off her feet.

"Whoa," Adelaide whispered. She looked down at her hands. Had *she* done that?

The dining hall was still again.

A fork clattered to the floor.

Becky's mouth dropped open as she searched for words, at last issuing a shriek so loud and pitiful it sounded animal. Chaos took over as Becky's dutiful followers rushed to her aid. Adelaide searched the floor in bewilderment. Her own lunch still lay in a puddle at her feet. But if she didn't throw the steak, who did? She scanned the crowd for an answer. In the very back stood the scowling Maggie Borland, wiping her soiled hands on her wrinkled jumper.

Adelaide wanted to thank her, but then Miss Patricia—large and square like an icebox—charged to the center of the dining hall and blew her whistle. Miss Patricia was in charge of the Elevens and Twelves dorm, gym class, and enforcement of all rules, and she rarely said anything without including the whistle.

"Maggie Borland and Adelaide Foss!" she yelled.

Adelaide didn't even have to hear the rest.

"That should do it!" said Mr. Zoethout, and he gently kicked one corner of his stand just to make sure it was stable.

"It looks good, Mr. Z!" said Steffen, standing back to admire his handiwork. He hadn't done all that much, really. Mostly, he'd just held up some stakes while Mr. Zoethout drove them into the dirt, but it felt nice to be needed. Doing a man's work, his dad would call it.

Mr. Zoethout's Candy Time stand stuck out like a bright, gleaming splinter in the middle of dull, brown Widowsbury Park. Its counter was painted in pink and white stripes to match the owner's apron. Dozens of glass canisters glistened with their sugary contents. Casting a shadow over the whole setup was a huge sign that announced the stand in a shocking rainbow of cotton-candy pastels. It certainly caught attention. People all around the park were staring at the construction with the same look one normally reserves for suspiciously smelly milk.

"I hope you're able to get some business," said Steffen.

"Nothing to worry about there. I've got it all planned," said Mr. Zoethout, polishing a jar of gum balls. "First, I'll send sample boxes to all the shops in town. Maybe they'll share some with their customers, and then—"

"I don't think that's such a good idea, Mr. Z," Steffen interrupted.

"Why not?" asked Mr. Zoethout.

Steffen pointed to the people watching them now, most of whom immediately turned away again. One mother gave them an unfriendly glare before pulling her child closer.

"You're new," said Steffen in a hushed voice. "People here don't like new. They get upset when you part your hair on a different side, let alone when you come from another town! Let alone when you come in on the Midnight!"

"You know, it might have been the eleven o'clock train, now that I think about it . . . ," said Mr. Zoethout.

"My point is that you're not from around here," said Steffen. "Just for that, they'll think you're trouble waiting to happen. But you can prove 'em wrong if you stick around long enough. It's just not gonna be overnight. You see?"

Mr. Zoethout's smile faded, and he nodded seriously. Then he brightened and reached out to shake Steffen's hand.

"Thanks again for the help, Steffen Weller. You're a good man," he said.

Steffen beamed with pride.

"Welcome to Widowsbury, Mr. Z!" he said, and he skipped all the way home, not even noticing the disapproving head shakes his townspeople gave him.

The library.

It was one of the darkest, coldest, most depressing rooms in all of Madame Gertrude's. Its gray stone walls were perpetually damp. The smell of mildew choked the air. And there was always the faint sound of something dripping, but nobody had ever been able to find the source. Adelaide had heard the library was a dungeon before the cathedral became a girls' school. She imagined the massive wooden bookshelves were once torture racks, repurposed to hold encyclopedias.

She tried to think of something more pleasant as she waited at her assigned table in the front right corner. Maggie sat in the back. Beatrice was there, too, dwarfed by her own table in the middle. This was how they always sat. They'd been in detention so many times there was a seating chart.

The library door swung open. Preceded by the telltale scent of oranges was Miss Delia and a massive stack of manila folders. The librarian dumped the folders onto her desk, producing a cloud of dust that made her cough. Then she cracked her knuckles, pulled a loose strand of hair behind her ear, adjusted the butterfly pin in her hair, and turned around.

"Hi," she said.

There was a long, uncomfortable silence as the prisoners watched their dungeon master.

"I'm Miss Delia," she added, bouncing a little on her heels.

She waited for several seconds, and when no one spoke, she grabbed a folder from the top of her stack.

"I understand that you're all here for detention," said Miss Delia from behind the folder. "Can anybody tell me why?"

No one answered, of course. Whenever past librarians asked a question, it was usually rhetorical.

"Anybody?" Miss Delia persisted.

Beatrice raised her hand enthusiastically. "Miss Anne said that I scare her in reading class, but I only wanted to know how Peter Pan might die if he ever could," she answered in her tiny voice. "That's only today, though. I don't remember about yesterday."

"I've been coming here so long, I don't remember why anymore," said Adelaide.

Maggie just scowled.

Miss Delia replaced the folder and sat on the edge of her desk with an exasperated sigh, which sent a wisp of her hair floating up.

"This is awkward," she said. Then, thinking for a second, she added, "Would anyone like to ask *me* any questions?"

Beatrice raised her hand again. "May I ask what you're going to do to us today?" she asked.

"Do . . . to you?"

"Yesterday I had to write 'I will not encourage spectral apparitions' one hundred times, but I didn't spell it right, so I had to do it one hundred more times and Mrs. Merryweather got very annoyed and then I had to help Adelaide and Maggie do the mopping," Beatrice clarified.

"Well . . . I . . . that is, nobody told me . . . ," said Miss Delia.

"Yes," said Adelaide. "Are you going to make us stand with dictionaries on our heads? Or rap us on the hands with a ruler if we look up?"

"Why would I make you do that? That's awful!" said Miss Delia. "And a terrible misuse of a dictionary, besides!"

"Then what are we to do, please? I don't want to get the ruler. It's made me afraid of math," Beatrice said with a pout.

Miss Delia blinked.

"Well, I thought we would . . . read," she answered.

Maggie burst out laughing.

"Read?!" she jeered. "In the library! That's stupid."

Miss Delia looked utterly baffled.

"Oh, I see. You're being funny, aren't you?" she said with a nervous laugh. "Aren't you?"

"That's not really what the library is for, Miss Delia," said Beatrice in a motherly tone. "I should know. I've been coming here every day since I was six years old. Sometimes I think I shall die here."

"You're only seven," Miss Delia pointed out.

"I know. It's very tragic," Beatrice sighed.

Miss Delia paused, scratched her arm, and adjusted her glasses. Then she hummed a few notes and made an odd clicking sound with her tongue.

I think this one's broken, thought Adelaide.

"I have an idea," Miss Delia said finally. "Why don't we get to know each other a little? Your headmistress says you'll be here every day, and if you're to be here every day, I should like to know something about you."

Maggie snorted.

"What's so funny about that?" said Miss Delia. "I thought, seeing as how you never get any recess, we'd go outside."

"But we're not allowed outside," Beatrice whispered.

"Mrs. Merryweather gave me permission to discipline you however I choose," said Miss Delia. "Anyway, I'm sure nobody would

23

mind just this once. It's just that this room is making me itch terribly and—and—"

She sneezed violently and shook her head, which made the wings on her butterfly pin wobble.

"—and I saw a lovely park up the road only this morning."

Adelaide couldn't remember the last time she'd gone outside. It must have been before she started school here. Was this a trap?

"But we must strike a bargain," said Miss Delia. "I'm new here, you know. Not only to your school, but to your town. Your headmistress told me you would all try to frighten me away! I would like to improve her impression of you. So, I'll tell you what. If you promise to be nice to me, I promise to be nice to you."

Adelaide eyed her warily. So far, the new librarian appeared to be almost . . . nice. She hadn't yet called any of them names like "brat" or "freak" or "insolent mutant." She hadn't made any threats. It seemed there was hope in this one, but then Adelaide's hopes had been dashed so many times before.

"Okay," she said cautiously.

"I promise!" said Beatrice cheerfully.

Maggie shrugged, which was the closest thing to agreement anyone could expect from her.

Sullen clouds held their breath over Widowsbury while Miss Delia and the girls made the trek to the park. There was no breeze to disturb the bloomless thistles that afternoon. There would be no tumbling for the tumbleweeds that had once been a prizewinning hedgerow. The only sounds were those of arguing crows, and of passersby shuffling to avoid the outsider and her strange young charges.

"What a lovely place to go for a walk!" Miss Delia remarked, though in reality, Widowsbury Park was not lovely at all. It was a vast field of dead grass, marred here and there by long-dead trees, some blackened by lightning. There was one worm-eaten bench near the entrance and a rusty old swing set no one ever approached, an unofficial monument to children lost many years ago. But Miss Delia didn't know the history of her new home. To her, this was simply a crisp December afternoon.

"What sort of books do you three like?" asked Miss Delia when they had seated themselves under the branches of a naked oak tree. "Surely, you do *some* reading in the library."

"Oh! Me! I like romantic stories!" Beatrice cheeped. "My mother gave me a book of fairy tales once, and I read 'Thumbelina' twenty times! Even though I felt sad for the mole."

"I like detective stories," Adelaide answered, once she was certain she was allowed. "Except I usually figure them out before the detective does."

Maggie spat out the blade of dead grass she'd been chewing. "I think books are a waste of time," she grumbled.

"What a shame, Maggie! We'll have to do something about that," said Miss Delia. "I like scary ones myself. There's nothing like frightening yourself silly with monsters right before bedtime, especially if there's a warm fire nearby."

Adelaide rolled an ancient acorn husk around in the dirt, contemplating whether or not she should speak her mind.

"I don't like those stories very much," she said at last.

"Oh?" said Miss Delia.

"I always feel bad for the monsters," Adelaide continued. "They're just lonely, most of them. Who wouldn't be when everybody calls you ugly and hunts you down all the time?"

Miss Delia looked troubled. "Yes," she said thoughtfully. "Yes, I see what you mean. I suppose that's one of the things that make them truly frightening, though. We're all afraid of something, but we've felt like the monsters, too."

"Some of us *are* the monsters," said Adelaide, and she thumped the acorn across the ground.

"That isn't true! I'd wager you've just had a rough start to the school year," said Miss Delia.

"I'm afraid it's much worse than that, Miss Delia," said Beatrice, "but we couldn't possibly expect you to understand."

"What about your friends, then?" the librarian said innocently. "Surely, they don't think you're monsters."

Adelaide looked away, stung. "What friends?" she said. "I don't have any."

"I'm not the kind of person anyone makes friends with. Not people, anyway," Beatrice said sadly.

Maggie threw a pebble at some gawkers in the distance.

"Aren't you even friends with each other?" asked Miss Delia.

Adelaide blushed, ashamed of her own snobbery.

"They don't usually let us talk in detention," she mumbled.

Miss Delia frowned. "I see," she said. "What would you say, then, if I asked you to be friends with me?"

Beatrice's mouth fell open. "But you're a librarian!"

"Doesn't mean I'm not allowed any friends," said Miss Delia, but then she glanced up and gasped. A few feet away was a tall sign over a small refreshment stand. IT'S ALWAYS TIME FOR CANDY! read the brightly colored sign, which resembled a wall clock with not enough numbers.

"Good heavens, what time is it?" said Miss Delia, jumping to her feet. "I've got to get the three of you back for classes!"

"My trusty pocket watch here tells me it's 12:55 in the afternoon, ma'am," said a man in a pink-and-white-striped apron behind the Candy Time stand.

"Thank you, sir!" said Miss Delia as she ushered the girls along.

"Name's Zoethout, ma'am. Lyle Zoethout!" he called after her with a bright smile and a tip of his hat. "Say! Won't you take a treat for your young friends before you go?"

Miss Delia stopped.

"I'm not sure I've got any money with me," she said, blushing.

"Now, don't you worry yourself about that," said Mr. Zoethout with a wink. "You're one of exactly two people to so much as smile at me since I got started today. In fact, people around here don't seem to think much of me or my stand at all, which is a shame because this licorice is really something. These are for you and the little ladies, with my compliments."

He swiftly prepared a small package of strawberry licorice and grinned as he held it over the counter.

"At least try it," he pleaded.

Miss Delia accepted the package and politely sampled a piece.

"This is very kind of you," she said. "I'm not sure what to say!"

There was something funny about her voice when she talked to him, and she was blinking a lot. Adelaide noticed the older girls do the same thing whenever they bumped into boys from the other school. It was embarrassing to watch.

"Just say you'll stop by my stand again," said the candy man, his green eyes twinkling. This made Miss Delia blink and blush even more.

"Miss Delia," said Adelaide, "shouldn't we be going? The teachers will be coming back from recess by now."

"Oh dear! You're right! Thank you, Mr. Zoethout! We have to be going now!" said Miss Delia. She pocketed the bag of treats. Then she took Beatrice's hand and ran, with Adelaide and Maggie right behind her.

"See you around!" Mr. Zoethout called after them, but Miss Delia could not hear him. A crowd of boys from Rudyard School had gathered in the park for a game of rugby, and they were shouting and cheering all at once. But Adelaide heard something else buried in the commotion.

"Someone help me!"

It was a woman's voice, hoarse from shouting.

"My son is gone! Have you seen Cornelius? Cornelius, come back! Oh, someone help me! HELP ME!"

The voice sent chills down Adelaide's back, but she brushed the feeling aside and kept running.

Somebody will help her, she thought. *Somebody who won't get in trouble for it.*

The girls and Miss Delia ran as fast as their legs would take them. They ran until it hurt to breathe. But for all their running, they were simply too late. Mrs. Merryweather was waiting for them when they returned. Beside her stood Becky Buschard.

"There. You see?" Becky was saying. "I thought I saw them leave the grounds, but I didn't think *those* girls were allowed to go anywhere. Was I wrong, Mrs. Merryweather?"

"No, my dear," Mrs. Merryweather seethed, "you were not."

- CHAPTER TWO -

Twelve Is an Unlucky Number

Mrs. Merryweather kept her eyes locked on Miss Delia.

"Ladies, go on to your classes," she said.

Becky sauntered off with a smirk on her face. Maggie started after her, but someone tugged at her sleeve. *No,* Beatrice mouthed.

"Go on, ladies!" Mrs. Merryweather repeated. But Adelaide was not going on to her classes. As soon as she was out of the headmistress's earshot, she turned and slipped down a different hallway.

"Wait!" said Beatrice. Maggie ran along beside her.

"What are you doing? Go to your classes and leave me alone," said Adelaide.

"But where are *you* going?" Beatrice whispered.

"To the library. I want to hear this, and nobody will see me there."

Beatrice was confused. "The library is on the other side of the school!" she said. "How can you hear anything from there? Won't we get in trouble?"

"Nobody's making you come along," said Adelaide.

But of course they went along. After all, what was the difference? It wouldn't be the first time they were late for their classes, and they were already bound for detention as it was. There was only one problem. The library door wouldn't budge.

"Of all the times!" Adelaide groaned.

"Phillip says it's locked," said Beatrice.

"Who's Phillip?" asked Adelaide, but Beatrice simply patted her front pocket closed and pretended not to hear.

Adelaide sighed. "Well, anyway, we're not getting in. So much for that plan," she said.

"Weak," Maggie muttered under her breath. Pushing between the other two, she grabbed the iron door handle and squeezed. There was a squealing sound as the handle warped, crunched, and eventually gave way. With a grunt that was more from annoyance than effort, she kicked open the heavy door as if it were made of cardboard.

"Um . . . thanks?" said Adelaide.

Inside, they hid behind the door as Adelaide pressed her ear to the wall.

"Ooh," she said. "Merryweather's furious!"

Maggie's brow furrowed.

"I can't hear anything," Beatrice whispered.

"It's not my fault if everyone in this school is deaf as a post. Now hush!" said Adelaide.

She concentrated, ignoring the sounds of termites munching up the walls, the pencil-writing of students in nearby classrooms, and the swirling of dust through the air vents. She didn't like what she heard.

"Miss Peet, I thought I made the rules perfectly clear to you," Mrs. Merryweather was saying. "Those girls are Trouble with a capital *T*, and they absolutely must . . . have . . . discipline!"

"I apologize, Mrs. Merryweather, but I simply don't understand why . . . ," began Miss Delia.

Mrs. Merryweather laughed unpleasantly.

"Why?!" she said. "Can you not see why? Those girls are everything a proper young lady should not be! Everything they are is strange! Or didn't Miss Alfred show you her collection of eulogies for deceased rats?"

"You write speeches about rats?" Adelaide asked Beatrice.

"They had nobody to mourn them. It made me feel sad," Beatrice mumbled. "What's Mrs. Merryweather saying?"

Adelaide pressed her ear to the wall again.

"I realize you're a newcomer here, but this is an extremely serious error in judgment, and it makes me question the validity of your references!" Mrs. Merryweather went on shouting.

"She's tearing Miss Delia to pieces for defending us," Adelaide reported. "She says we're going to ruin this school's name, and Miss Delia will be responsible."

"But we were only outside for a little while!" cried Beatrice.

" 'Meant for the best,' did you? I doubt that," Mrs. Merryweather was saying now. "If you really meant for the best, you would have followed the rules I have laid down for you instead of questioning my experience in these matters! I should have expected this from you. 'Don't bring in an outsider!' they all told me, but after all the librarians those three had driven off before, I felt I had no choice!"

"Oh, come on. That just isn't fair!" said Adelaide.

There had, in fact, been eleven librarians prior to Miss Delia. Few had lasted longer than a week. All but one of them cited fear of the three girls as reasons for their prompt departures. The exception was old Mrs. Ethel, who was so mean that she gave herself an embolism and was advised by her doctor either to be a little kinder or retire. She left immediately.

"What's not fair? Adelaide, what are they saying? Maggie, can you hear them?" Beatrice whined. Maggie cupped a hand to the wall, listened, and shook her head.

"Would you please be quiet?" Adelaide hissed.

Miss Delia's voice was weaker now. "I didn't realize it was as serious as that," she said.

"Of course you didn't! Stranger!" Mrs. Merryweather spat. "Don't make yourself too comfortable here, Miss Peet. I am warning you. If you break my rules one more time, you will be let go posthaste!"

With that, Mrs. Merryweather stormed down the hall. For several seconds, Adelaide heard nothing but Miss Delia's labored breathing— the sound of someone trying not to cry. Then Miss Delia stomped her foot, sending a *clack!* reverberating through the walls.

"Ow!" cried Adelaide. She fell back and massaged her ear.

"What happened? What *happened?*" Beatrice begged.

Adelaide, still holding her ear, frowned.

"She said that if Miss Delia is nice to us again, she's going to fire her."

"Oh no!" said Beatrice.

"I guess it's back to the usual," said Adelaide. Then she heard something else. Footsteps. They were still a long way off, but they were headed for the library.

"Someone's coming!" she warned.

Adelaide buried herself in the corner behind the door. Maggie darted behind a bookshelf. Beatrice tried several places unsuccessfully before sliding under Miss Delia's desk.

Click. Clack. Click. Clack. Click! Clack! went the footsteps for what felt like an eternity until at last they stopped at the door. Adelaide forgot to breathe as the mangled handle rattled loosely, some of its screws leaping to the floor with a delicate *ping*. She squeezed her eyes shut and prepared herself for the worst. If Mrs. Merryweather discovered they had deliberately disobeyed her! Well, they'd get detention. Again. But it could get worse. There was a place she could take them. A place so cruel it was rarely even threatened. Adelaide shuddered at the thought.

Not Mrs. Merryweather! Not Mrs. Merryweather! Not Mrs. Merryweather! she hoped.

Luck was on her side just this once, for it was not Mrs. Merryweather who opened the door but a weary Miss Delia. Her eyes were red, her face was blotchy, and she looked as if all the joy had gone out of her.

She eyed the screws on the floor. She pulled back the door and looked behind it. Then she stared at Adelaide in confusion.

"What in the world are you doing back there? And what happened to the door handle?" she asked.

"I—I—I don't know," Adelaide stuttered, playing with her braids. "We—I wanted to ask you . . . if . . . you were all right!"

"There was a 'we' in there," said Miss Delia.

Maggie and Beatrice popped out from their hiding places.

"We thought we might've gotten you into trouble," Beatrice said. "I know what it's like to be in trouble, and I wouldn't wish it on anyone else."

Maggie shrugged as if to agree that this was more or less true.

"I'll be fine," said Miss Delia with a tired smile. "I suppose tomorrow we'd best stay inside and stick to reading, then, huh? I'm afraid I've made a mess of things."

"It's not you, Miss Delia. It's us," said Beatrice.

"Nonsense," Miss Delia scoffed. "Why would you say that? I'm the one who broke the rules, after all. I'm sure Mrs. Merryweather understands."

But Adelaide shook her head. "That's not what she means," she said. "Mrs. Merryweather doesn't like us. Nobody likes us. If *you* like us, that means you're different from everybody else, and that drives Mrs. Merryweather crazy! You have to fit in if you want to stay here, Miss Delia. Take it from me."

Miss Delia looked at the girls, who each stared despondently at the floor.

"Oh, you poor children," she murmured sadly.

Then she remembered the time and cleared her throat. "Well," she said, smoothing the wrinkles out of her skirt. "I may be new around here, but I'm sure it's not as bad as all that. Everyone has difficult days, and they don't last forever! But I know what it's like to have those days, and I want you to know that you can always count on me to listen. Now, you'd better go on to your classes before Mrs. Merryweather catches you! I'll see you right here tomorrow."

"Yes, Miss Delia," said the three, and they made their way out the door.

Just before Adelaide left the library, she stopped and turned toward the librarian.

"Thanks," she said quietly.

Miss Delia nodded in understanding.

Adelaide's dreams that night were feverish and filled with things she didn't like to think about.

"What about your friends? What about your friends? *What about your friends?*" she heard in Miss Delia's voice.

"I don't have any friends," she said in her sleep.

"You could be friends with me," said Miss Delia.

"Do you mean that?" asked Adelaide, but before Miss Delia could answer, the librarian evaporated into a puff of smoke and was replaced by Mrs. Merryweather.

"You'll never have any friends, you scary child," she said. "Your parents rode in here on a wave of bad luck, and you'll only bring more problems for everyone!"

"But I'm not scary! I'm not!" Adelaide protested.

She bolted upright in her bed, gasping for air. The room was silent apart from the snores of her classmates in the Elevens and Twelves dormitory.

A shape moved in the darkness.

"*Beatrice!*" she whispered.

Beatrice was sitting on the floor beside Adelaide's bed, wide-eyed and clutching a stuffed toy mouse.

"Thank heaven!" she said softly. "I was afraid the Other Ghosts would come if I waited much longer!"

"Other ghosts? Beatrice, what are you doing here? This isn't even your floor! If you wake everyone up, I'll never live it down!" said Adelaide as quietly as she could.

"I had an idea," Beatrice whispered, "but I'm not very good at spelling, and Maggie won't tell me what she wants it to say."

Across the room, Maggie grunted and pulled her blanket over her head.

"What she wants what to say?" Adelaide asked.

Beatrice slid a piece of folded green paper and some crayons onto the bed. The paper said "We r sorey" on the front.

"I made a 'sorry' card for Miss Delia. She was so nice to us today, and then she got in trouble with Mrs. Merryweather, and I just feel awful about it. Nobody's ever nice to us, have you noticed?"

"Yeah. Somewhat," Adelaide said dryly.

"I wanted to surprise her with it in the morning, but I don't know what else to write," said Beatrice.

Adelaide fell back onto her pillow and groaned.

"All right. Fine," she grumbled. "I'll write something. But I need some time, okay?"

Beatrice nodded.

"And *I'll* give it to her during breakfast. You're little and clumsy, so you'll just get caught. Then we'll all be in trouble."

Beatrice nodded.

"So . . . ? Go back to the little kids' floor before somebody catches you here!"

Beatrice nodded again. Then she realized that was an instruction, and she scrambled to her feet.

Adelaide looked around to see if anyone was watching her. Then she took a crayon and began to write.

Miss Delia paced up and down the floor of her modest room, sipping her warm milk as she walked. Try as she might, the sleepy feeling would not come. This day had simply been too upsetting. She hated first days for a reason, and today had been the worst of firsts. She'd only been trying to help, after all, and she'd certainly never had her job threatened before. On the surface, this school was a lovely place. Underneath all that was something that left a bad taste in her mouth.

Miss Delia slid open her small window and breathed in the cool night air. The sky was mottled with moonlight and clouds, but where there were gaps, the stars twinkled in a friendly way. *Like Mr. Zoethout's eyes,* she thought. She sighed and closed the window.

"A walk," she said to herself. That was just the thing. A good stroll always made everything right as rain. Miss Delia pulled on her overcoat and locked her door. Then she descended the steps from the teachers' quarters to the main hall, stopping once to make a face at the bust of Madame Gertrude.

IN HONOR OF MADAME GERTRUDE VON TRUDERHEIM. MAY YOU

TEACH THE ANGELS A LESSON AS YOU TAUGHT US said a brass plaque beneath it.

"Go teach *yourself* a lesson, you old goat!" said Miss Delia.

Outside, she headed up the road to Widowsbury Park. Just ahead of her, a window over one of the shops turned yellow with light. She waved politely at the silhouette that watched her, but the silhouette immediately drew the curtains, and then the light went out.

While Miss Delia walked, her thoughts returned to the candy man. Such a charming smile! And those brilliant green eyes—they were like two gemstones under his boyish hair. He hadn't minded at all that she was newly arrived. "Just say you'll stop by my stand again," he'd said. Did he mean that?

A sudden chill interrupted her thoughts. Miss Delia slipped her hands into her overcoat pockets, where she was surprised to find the strawberry licorice Mr. Zoethout had given her earlier. She had almost forgotten it, but it made for a perfect addition to her soothing stroll. As she enjoyed the sticky sweet candy, she wondered if Mr. Zoethout liked to take walks, too. She imagined stumbling into him. *Oh, I'm so sorry!* she'd say. *Not at all, miss. It's a pleasure*, he'd say as he helped her to her feet. And then he'd take her hand, and . . .

Where in the world am I? she thought, and she realized with alarm that the park was nowhere in sight. A shiver passed through her as she looked around in a panic. Somehow she had wandered off into the woods. It was so very dark without the warmth of lamplight, and so very cold. And now she wasn't even sure which direction she'd come from.

Just ahead of her, she made out the shape of something tall and skeletal. Some sort of building, it appeared. She moved toward it and found it to be—of all the things in the world!—a carousel.

"What are you doing all the way out here?" Miss Delia said aloud. Here in the dark, she almost expected it to answer her. No one had told her of any carousels in Widowsbury, but what a nice surprise after an upsetting day, she thought.

She climbed up onto the creaky wooden platform and ran her hand over one of the braided poles. From what she could see in the darkness, the carousel appeared to have been abandoned for some time. It was a wonder it stood at all, the way it leaned and sagged under the weight of its canopy. She could see that some of the metal horses had lost their painted eyes to patches of rust. And they were posed so dramatically—some of them with their heads twisted the wrong way around.

But something about this peculiar finding comforted her. Her aunt and uncle used to take her to the fair when she was small, and she had always loved the carousel. It was quite different from this one, of course. That one had beautiful flying unicorns, and everything sparkled like stardust.

Suddenly she heard all around her a skittering sound like a swarming army of insects. It grew so loud she found herself brushing away these invisible insects, until she realized where the sound was coming from.

The rust. The rust was creeping away from the carousel.

The more Miss Delia's eyes became accustomed to the darkness, the more she noticed other things changing, too. The faded paint grew steadily brighter. The scratched gilt seemed to rep. itself right in front of her.

"I'm dreaming. That's what this is," said Miss Delia. Except it didn't feel like a dream.

She heard a crackling and then a buzzing sound as the once-shattered lightbulbs repaired themselves and glowed with life. They chased around the edge of the canopy and then the floor until the carousel was one dazzling blaze of light. When the familiar organ music began blaring—*WomPAH! WomPAH! WomPAH! Dee-deeeeee doo deedle-dee!*—Miss Delia was sure this was a dream. The horse nearest her wriggled like a serpent shedding its skin, and a horn sprouted from its forehead, as did a pair of wings from its sides. Before her very eyes, the carousel was transforming into the exact one she remembered!

Well, if this is a dream, I'm going to enjoy it, Miss Delia thought. Then she threw one leg over the unicorn's back, and the ride began to revolve. Slowly at first, then faster and faster still. Night faded into daylight. Leafless trees melted away to reveal stalls of cows with prize ribbons on their sides. On the air she smelled her aunt's famous apple pie.

"Come on! Come on!" Miss Delia commanded with a laugh. "Go faster!"

And it did.

The following morning saw Adelaide, Maggie, and Beatrice tip-toeing down the stairs to the main hall. But Adelaide was not at all pleased.

"I thought I told you not to come along," she grumbled, her face as cloudy as the Widowsbury sky.

"I'm sorry, Adelaide! I forgot!" said Beatrice.

"And then you had to go and get Maggie," Adelaide snapped. "If we get caught, Mrs. Merryweather's going to think we've formed a gang."

"Probably," Maggie agreed, though the idea of it didn't seem to bother her much.

"I just thought the door might be locked again or something. Oh, I hope I haven't ruined everything!" Beatrice said, worried.

Adelaide stopped and held up her hand. "I hear someone!" she hissed.

Around the corner from the bottom of the staircase, the gardener was gossiping to the janitor.

"Didja hear about the Patterson kid? Been missing since yesterday," he was saying. There was a rustle of newspaper pages.

"Oh," said the janitor. "Have they got any leads?"

Adelaide heard the gardener hum to himself as he flipped through the paper.

"The *Herald* says, 'Cornelius Patterson Jr. was last seen by his mother, Caroline Patterson, yesterday afternoon in Widowsbury Park. He was wearin' a bright yellow sweater and a blue cap. More information is expected to be available when Mrs. Patterson recovers from severe shock.' Doesn't sound like they know anything else," said the gardener. "Speakin' of . . . have you heard from Elmer?"

"Nah," said the janitor.

Beatrice tapped on Adelaide's shoulder. "Aren't we going to be late? What are they talking about? I can't quite hear—" she whispered, but was interrupted by Adelaide's hand over her mouth.

Adelaide pointed impatiently to her own ear and went back to listening.

"It's the gardener. And the janitor, I think. They're talking about the news," she said. "Some people have gone missing, it sounds like. Elmer Whitley and a little boy."

"Strangest thing," the gardener was saying. "He'd better turn up soon. He left his truck out by the park, and they've gone and towed it up to the yard. If you ask me, Elmer's probably hidin' till ol' Merryweather steps off her warpath. Can't say I wouldn't do the same. Did you know she hired an outsider?"

"No!" said the janitor.

"Whole town's talkin' about it! Librarian from Burgtown. Arrived yesterday, which—if you'll recall—was the twelfth day of the twelfth month, which makes it the twelfth anniversary of the Big Storm. That's three twelves in a row. Bad luck, I'd say," the gardener went on. "You know, I just don't trust nobody who'd come here of their own free will when most of us would leave if we could. Must be a dandy thing to come and go as you please. No such luck for those of us who've been here since before the Storm. Can't even cross town limits."

"No sir," the janitor agreed, and went back to mopping.

"Never mind. Now they're just being rude about Miss Delia,"

Adelaide grumbled. She motioned for her companions to follow as she carefully sneaked down the rest of the stairs and darted past the corner.

"Eh, watch out. It's the weirdy brigade," she heard the gardener say, and then, "Hey! Where do you weirdies think you're going?"

"Ignore them. Go! Go!" Adelaide commanded, and they hurried down through the main hall, followed by the gardener's boisterous laughter.

"I really don't like that man," said Adelaide when they reached the library.

"He's probably very lonely inside. Phillip says he—never mind," Beatrice said.

Maggie rolled her eyes and shoved open the library door, the handle of which was now missing entirely.

"None of it matters as long as Miss Delia likes our card—" Adelaide began. But it was not Miss Delia they found in the library.

Mrs. Merryweather towered over them with a sneer, her bony arms folded tight across her chest.

"Miss Borland, Miss Alfred, and Miss Foss," she said, pronouncing each name as if it were a disgusting medical diagnosis. "What, pray tell, brings you here when Breakfast Time is about to begin?"

The girls were unable to speak. The card fell from Adelaide's hand, but before she could pick it back up, Mrs. Merryweather snatched it.

" 'Miss Delia,' " she read. " 'We . . . are . . . sorry?' I can tell by the atrocious spelling which part is yours, Miss Alfred. 'It's our fault

Mrs. Merryweather yelled at you. You're very nice. We will understand if you have to pretend not to be to keep your job. Your friends: Beatrice A., Maggie B., and Adelaide F.' Isn't that touching? If only you weren't altogether too late."

Mrs. Merryweather crumpled the card into a green wad and crammed it into her pocket. Beatrice cried out before she could stop herself.

"You've fired her!" Adelaide yelled.

"No," Mrs. Merryweather said coolly. "She couldn't handle her responsibilities, so she left in the night. We are again without a librarian for you three to terrorize!"

"I don't believe you!" said Adelaide.

"I don't give a hoot what you believe, Miss Foss! The fact remains that we are rid of that woman and her careless ways, and I, for one, am glad of it!" Mrs. Merryweather thundered.

"Now," she added in a low voice, "go back to the dining hall and sit in your places for the Breakfast Lecture before I lose my patience!"

Maggie and Beatrice backed toward the door. Adelaide's blood was boiling. She could *hear* it boiling.

"I'm going to find out what really happened to Miss Delia," she said as they hurried to the dining hall. Hot tears stung her eyes, but she'd bite her own arm off before she'd let them show.

"But Mrs. Merryweather said—" Beatrice started.

"Mrs. Merryweather is a witch," Adelaide snapped, "and if you believe everything she says, you're just as bad as that rat Becky."

She ran to her place before anyone could see her cry.

Beatrice stopped, her brow furrowed. "She didn't mean what she said about rats just now, did she?" she asked Maggie, but Maggie wasn't listening. She was watching Becky Buschard, intent burning in her eyes.

Behind the dining hall of Madame Gertrude's, Steffen Weller stood on a stack of fruit crates and peered into the garbage bin. His eyes ran over its contents, searching for a specific something. He'd gotten a book about inventing things for his birthday, and all he needed was one simple part. It was supposed to be common, but he wasn't having the best luck finding one, and he had already searched everywhere at Rudyard.

"Phooey!" he said, but then something else caught his eye. It was a leather suitcase. Black. Magazine flowers pasted to its sides.

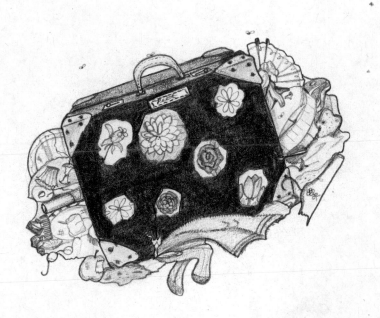

- Chapter Three -
The Smell of Fear

It was a sunless morning. Of course, the same could be said for every morning. For the past twelve years, the weather in the Pernicious Valley had been locked at a permanent forty-eight degrees Fahrenheit. The skies were always gray in Widowsbury, and every season was just autumn all over again.

But there were days when the wind stirred the bone-dry tree leaves in such a way that it sounded like whispers of warning. When the shadows were longer than they ought to be, and a man looked at his neighbor with more suspicion than usual. They called it the Dread, and today it was especially strong.

The only thing Henry Fernberger II felt, however, was the overwhelming wish to do something bad. He'd done almost all a boy could do, but it wasn't easy to upset people when one's parents were as important as the Fernbergers. So, today he was going to skip school entirely. Everyone would worry about where he'd gone and if his parents would find out. The teachers would all be so steamed they'd want to yell at him when he came back, but they wouldn't be able to say a thing!

Just the thought of it made Henry laugh out loud as he boldly strolled out of Rudyard School's front doors.

On the stoop, Henry saw the familiar white-blond hair of the cook's son. Steffen Weller was on his knees, arranging a set of twigs. Probably building something weird again. Freak.

"If it ain't Welly!" Henry said with a sneer.

Steffen looked up, squinted, and then went back to building his stick contraption. There were tangled strings of dental floss mixed up in the mess, and a cracked custard dish with dirt all over it. Henry knelt beside Steffen and noticed a moth hole in the boy's coat. He smelled of stale peanut butter, too.

52

"What's that? An art project?" Henry asked.

Steffen shook his head.

"Aw, come on," said Henry. "I just want to know."

"It's an invention. I got a book about them for my birthday," Steffen answered meekly.

"Nice present if you're *poor*," said Henry.

He jumped to his feet and gave Steffen's contraption a kick, scattering twigs and floss all over the sidewalk.

"Oops!" he said. Steffen didn't even look up.

"See ya later, Welly!" said Henry, and he walked off down the street, snickering.

What an embarrassment Welly was with his scuffed-up shoes and hand-me-down sweaters. He didn't even go to school at Rudyard; he was taught at home—by his own father! In Henry's opinion, such people shouldn't be seen by the students, but then Henry would have one less person to torture, and that wouldn't be much fun.

His walk took him to Widowsbury Park, where he soon came by the brand-new Candy Time stand. Someone had defaced it since he'd seen it last. GO HOME STRANGER it said in green paint across the front of the counter.

"Hello there, sir!" said the candy man with a pretend salute. "Anything I can get for you today?"

Henry stopped dead in his tracks. His throat suddenly felt dry. *The newcomer.* For a brief moment, he considered turning back, but then he imagined what his friends would say when he told them how *he* faced the stranger alone . . . man to man! With that thought, Henry puffed out his chest and swaggered over. He pulled out a hefty pile of change with his chubby fingers and spilled it over the counter as messily as possible.

"Whatever that'll get me, as long as it's chocolate," he ordered.

He wanted to see the candy man try to count it all, but the man only pushed the money from the counter into his cash register without another glance.

"Got big plans today?" he asked Henry, filling a paper bag with various candies.

"Going up to the woods to catch some spiders," Henry answered gruffly.

"I hear you can find the biggest ones just beyond the park, where the trees start," said the candy man. "You know, those big black and yellow ones that crunch when you step on 'em. Of course, I wouldn't go in there myself. Lots of scary stories about those woods!"

"Who asked you? You're not even from our town," Henry snapped. He snatched the candy without so much as a thank-you, and ran away perhaps faster than he might have had anyone else been watching.

He made his way into Henbane Wood, chomping chocolate greedily as he went. With a large stick he found in the dirt, he took violent whacks at all the bushes. He liked stirring up all the critters that lived inside. Those big black and yellow spiders were his favorite. Of course, he wouldn't step on them. He'd collect them, sneak them into the girls' school, and then wait for the screams.

Whack! Nothing.

Whack! Some small, boring beetles.

Whack! Whack! Whack! Ping!

Henry's stick struck something hard and snapped in two. He looked up to see what had done the damage and was startled to find himself standing a hair's-breadth from the bared teeth of a large metal horse. Its eyes were scratched out and rusted over. A mealworm scuttled from a nostril.

"*Aaaaaaa!*" Henry shouted.

Oh, he thought when he looked again. *It's only an old carousel. Who put that here?*

It was a dark and ugly thing, this carousel. It appeared that someone had been painting it quite recently, but clearly they were far from finishing the job. *Stupid baby stuff,* he thought, and he spat a pitiful bubble of saliva into the dirt.

He was just about to continue his quest for spiders when he heard someone calling his name.

"*Henry! Hennnnnnryyyyyy!*"

The woman's voice sounded both familiar and strange, and it seemed to come from everywhere and yet nowhere all at once. Henry couldn't see her, but he noticed with an uncomfortable feeling in his stomach that she sounded just like his beloved nanny. The thing was, Nanny Harriet had died when he was seven. Henry was almost thirteen now.

"H-Harriet?"

He swatted at something crawling on his neck but found it was only his own hair.

"Harriet? Is that you?"

"Come and find me, Henry! It's been so long since we played a game!"

Now the voice seemed to be coming from the carousel. Henry climbed up its rotten wooden steps and looked around. Something inside him told him he shouldn't be there, but he ignored the feeling. No one told Henry he shouldn't do something. Not even himself.

"Where are you? They said you died of the fever!" he insisted. "I saw them put garlic flowers on you because they said you were . . . they said you . . ."

"They said I might come back?"

And just like that, Harriet was sitting on one of those metal horses, holding out her arms. She looked exactly as he remembered her from when he was small, so much so that he forgot to be afraid. His vision blurred with tears, and he was grateful none of his friends could see him now.

"I came back anyway," said Harriet. "They can't keep me from my little boy."

Henry wiped his nose on his jacket sleeve and jumped into his nanny's arms. He sobbed and told her all his troubles. Nothing had been the same since Harriet had passed away. Mother and Father sent him to Rudyard after that, and nobody read to him anymore. His parents rarely visited even though they lived just on the edge of town. They were simply too busy with their charities. Why hadn't she come back sooner?

"There, there," Harriet cooed. "There, there."

The ride began to spin slowly—so slowly that Henry didn't notice it at first. As it picked up speed, he started to feel all right again. There was nothing odd about his nanny coming back from the dead. Nothing strange about the sad music blaring from the calliope. It was wonderful, that's what it was! Just wonderful! Like he'd never had to grow up!

Except that everything was getting darker now. Life had come into the weird, half-painted horses, but they changed shape every time he blinked. Now they hissed and snapped like lizards. *This isn't fun anymore,* he thought. Henry tried to wrench himself free, but his nanny's fingers dug into his arms. He couldn't move, and he was wishing he hadn't eaten so much chocolate.

"Harriet, it's going too fast. I'm gonna be sick," he said groggily.

But Harriet wasn't Harriet anymore. Her hands had become talons, and her eyes were nothing but gaping holes.

"THERE, THERE," croaked the Harriet-thing.

Henry wanted to scream, but he felt so very tired all of a sudden. He could barely hold his eyes open.

"No . . . ," he whimpered.

Then the shadows closed in around him.

"Adelaide! Hey! Adelaide!"

"What?"

"Do you think maybe Mrs. Merryweather is hiding Miss Delia somewhere?"

"I don't want to talk about it, Beatrice."

"Oh. Okay. But . . . do you think she is?"

Adelaide turned to Beatrice. "Look, I don't want to be mean, but if people think we're friends, they're going to make fun of us even more than they already do," she said.

Beatrice looked down at her shoes and mumbled an apology.

It was recess time. With no one to watch them and no time for alternative plans, Mrs. Merryweather had permitted her Trio of Trouble to be outdoors for once.

"But don't expect this privilege twice!" she had threatened.

Adelaide closed her eyes for a few seconds and sniffed the air. It would rain soon. She could smell the clouds just waiting to burst.

"Oh no! It's the scary children! We'd better hide!" someone shouted from across the playground with much giggling.

"Yes, or Adelaide will *bite* us!" teased someone else. "Then we'll have no one to talk to but Beatrice's ghost friends!"

Adelaide opened her eyes and shook her head. "See? It's already started."

Beatrice began to cry, which made Adelaide feel rather ashamed of herself.

"Hey. I'm sorry. I didn't mean it. Really!" she said.

Beatrice rubbed the tears from her eyes and sniffled. "I would understand if you did," she said. "I wouldn't want to be friends with me, either."

"Aw, don't say that," said Adelaide. "I take it back, okay? Forget I said it. Tell me about your friend Phillip. Is he the one you're always talking to?"

Beatrice shrank back.

"You'll laugh at me."

"No, I won't! I promise!"

Beatrice bit her bottom lip and looked around to see if anybody else was listening. Then she leaned in close.

"He's a mouse."

"You keep a *mouse* in your pocket? Let me see!" said Adelaide, but Beatrice covered her pocket with her hands.

"You can't. He's dead," she whispered.

Adelaide scrunched her nose in disgust.

"No, no! It's not his body!" Beatrice explained. "The janitor got rid of that ages ago. Phillip's a ghost now. He's too shy to play with the other ghost mice, so he stays with me."

Adelaide raised an eyebrow in disbelief.

"He's my friend! I know lots of animals!" said Beatrice. "They're scared of us when they're alive, but after they're dead, they aren't scared anymore. They'll talk to you if you can see them. But I don't think very many people can."

"Uh-huh," said Adelaide. "So, do you talk to people ghosts, too?"

Beatrice's eyes grew large, and what little color she possessed drained rapidly from her face. "I won't talk to them. Never, never, never," she said softly.

"Won't or can't?"

"*I won't talk to them,*" she repeated. And that was that.

They walked over to Maggie, who hung upside down from the jungle gym she had just overtaken.

"May we?" asked Adelaide.

"Be my guest," said Maggie.

Adelaide perched herself on one of the bars. "I liked Miss Delia," she said.

"Me too," Beatrice agreed.

"Sometimes I think we really are 'scary children,'" said Adelaide. "I mean, what if she just quit like Merryweather said?"

"She wouldn't have!" Beatrice cried.

"Why not? Why shouldn't she be scared of us like everyone else?" said Adelaide. "My mom always says that people are afraid of anything different. She says it like it's something to be proud of, but I don't know anymore."

"My mother says I'm special!" piped Beatrice.

"My mom says that, too," said Adelaide. "I'm sick of being special."

"My ma says she's gonna ground me for the whole summer if she finds out I broke anything," said Maggie.

Adelaide and Beatrice stared at her.

"Too late," she added with a rare grin.

A low muttering of thunder issued from the darkening sky. The three girls looked up, searching for signs of interesting weather and, perhaps, for something to talk about. None of them were particularly accustomed to conversation.

"I still can't believe Miss Delia would've run off like that," said Beatrice at last. "She said she was warned about us. She said she wanted to be our friend anyway. And we had a perfectly nice time in the park yesterday until we got in trouble."

"There's the problem," said Adelaide. "It's one thing to deal with troublemakers—which I don't think we are. It's another thing to deal with your boss. Miss Delia got yelled at because of us on her very first day, and you should've heard the things Mrs. Merryweather said about us after that! Miss Delia must've thought we were criminal masterminds or something."

"If only," said Maggie.

"Besides. I've been doing some thinking since this morning," Adelaide continued, digging into the sand with the toe of her boot. "Even if she was fired . . . even if we somehow got to the bottom of it, how would we get her to come back? She's done for as a librarian. What's she going to do? Beg for her job?"

"We could stage a revolt," Maggie suggested without any hint of sarcasm.

"We could write letters to the mayor!" said Beatrice.

"Or we could forget she was ever here and just accept that people are never going to like us," said Adelaide.

Beatrice clucked her tongue and folded her arms across her chest, which made her look like an angry doll.

"Adelaide Foss, that is a terrible attitude to have at a time like this. What would Miss Delia say?" she scolded, her oversized bow bobbing with each motion of her head.

"Look, all I'm saying is . . . ," Adelaide began. She stopped and tilted her head to one side. "Hey, be quiet for a second."

From across the road came the sound of running feet. She sniffed the air again. Among the mixed smells of dirt and discarded lunches, she discerned the odor of panic and perspiration. She dropped to the ground and pressed her ear to it. The runner was wearing expensive shoes and a fancy suit. She could tell by the sound of the fabric hitting the backs of his calfskin—no—patent-leather oxfords.

"Goodness, Gregory, what on earth is the matter?" she heard Mrs. Merryweather say.

"One of my students has disappeared. He's been gone all morning," said the man in the fancy suit, who turned out to be the headmaster of Rudyard. "Miriam, it's the Fernberger boy!"

Beatrice crouched beside Adelaide. "What are you hearing?" she whispered.

"Mr. Edwin is talking to Mrs. Merryweather. Sounds like somebody else has gone missing," said Adelaide.

"Saints alive! Do his parents know?" Mrs. Merryweather was saying now.

"Not yet," said Mr. Edwin.

"Good. The amount of money they donate to our two institutions! Gregory, there's nothing for it!"

"Sounds serious," said Adelaide. She continued to listen. "They're talking about putting a search party together from *both* schools!"

She strained to hear the rest, but a shadow fell across her. She looked up with alarm and found herself under the scrutiny of Cordelia Minucci, Becky Buschard's best friend and chief emulator. Adelaide had been so focused on the sounds across the playground that she hadn't even heard Cordelia approach.

"Whatcha doing down there, Dog-Ears? Somebody blow a dog whistle?" asked Cordelia.

"She was listening to something *important,*" said Beatrice.

"N-no I wasn't. I dropped something in the sand. That's all. I—I was looking for it," Adelaide stuttered as she jumped to her feet and patted her braids in place. Beatrice frowned at the lie.

Behind them, Maggie dropped down from the jungle gym and stood upright.

"What if we drop *you* in the sand?" Maggie threatened Cordelia.

"What if *you* get a hairbrush?" Cordelia snapped back.

But now Maggie was cracking her knuckles, and that was all the warning Cordelia Minucci needed. Defeated, she harrumphed and stomped away.

"Are my ears showing?" Adelaide asked frantically.

"No, but your epidermis is."

"What?!" Adelaide cried.

"Never mind, it was a joke. What does it matter if your ears are showing?" asked Maggie, but Adelaide ignored her.

Mrs. Merryweather marched to the center of the playground and loudly clapped her hands.

"Ladies!" she called. "I want you all to return to the building and assemble in the auditorium in an orderly and ladylike fashion. Junior teachers, you will stay behind. Gather anyone else who isn't on the playground. We don't want anyone unaccounted for! Senior teachers, you will follow me, and I implore you to hurry!"

Above them, the gathering storm clouds turned coal black, tinged with a sickly green. Adelaide could feel the electricity of lightning not yet discharged. It was as powerful as the smell of fear.

"I feel like something very bad is happening," said Beatrice, patting her pocket protectively.

"The teachers are scared to death," said Adelaide. "Can't you smell it?"

"I'll take your word for it," said Maggie.

While the junior teachers strove to return order to the playground, the senior teachers formed a group behind Mrs. Merryweather. All of them watched the sky turning blacker by the second. Then the rain started, thick and oily and as cold as bones.

"It's happening again," a teacher said. "It's just like the Big Storm."

But then Mrs. Merryweather began to bark more instructions at them before Adelaide could learn anything more.

As the hunt commenced for the missing boy, gossip flooded the auditorium at Madame Gertrude's.

"I saw Mr. Edwin talking to Mrs. Merryweather. Think someone got caught kissing again?"

"Don't be stupid. Didn't you see the clouds? There's going to be another Storm!"

"We're going to be eaten by zombies!"

"No we're not. We've had normal storms since the Big One, you know."

"My grandfather says that's why they cremate people now. 'Cuz of the zombies."

Adelaide closed her eyes and focused on the sound of the rain drumming the roof until the swirling chatter blurred into one low hum. Whenever the noises grew too much to bear, she imagined she was standing on the deck of a clipper ship. Or any kind of ship, really, as long as it was sailing far away. Sometimes the wind made the rafters creak like an old boat, and she could almost smell the salty ocean spray, the damp wood, and the . . . peanut butter?

Adelaide opened her eyes. There, standing next to her, was a boy munching a peanut butter sandwich.

"Hi," said the boy. "Care for a sandwich?"

The boy looked exactly like pictures Adelaide had seen of street urchins in Dickens stories. He was short and scrawny, with bright blue eyes behind misshapen wire glasses. On his fair head he wore a dirty newsboy cap tilted just so. His patched wool coat was at least two sizes too large, and he carried a bulging knapsack from which poked a broken fishing pole with odd knickknacks hanging from its line.

"No thank you. I'm sorry, but who *are* you?" asked Adelaide.

"Oh, I'm Steffen Weller," said the peanut butter boy. "My dad's

the cook at Rudyard. I was supposed to bor-
row a cup of flour from your school's cook,
but somebody grabbed me and made me come
inside. Don't ask me why. They usually just
toss a whole bag of the stuff at me."

"That was probably a mistake, Steffen
Weller. I don't think you're supposed to be
here," said Adelaide.

Beatrice turned around and, upon seeing
Steffen, giggled behind her hands.

"What are *you* doing in here? You're a boy!"
she squeaked.

"It's not my fault I'm here!" Steffen sniffed.
"They made me! I don't ask questions! Sandwich?"

Beatrice politely declined. Maggie turned to see
what all the commotion was about, rolled her
eyes, and went back to looking bored with everything.

"Suit yourself. My dad says it's always good to have a sandwich
with you. Never know when you might need it," said Steffen.

He finished his lunch and pulled a knotted ball of kite string
from his knapsack, humming to himself as he made new knots
in it.

"I bet this is about a kid named Henry," he said. "I think he was
skipping class, but I wouldn't know for sure. I don't go to school.
Not officially."

"What do you mean you don't go to school? Everybody goes to school," said Adelaide.

"Not everybody can afford to go to Rudyard or *Madame Geeeer- trude's*," said Steffen, affecting a snobbish tone, "but that's the only choice you've got around here unless you want to fall down a hole in the ground like Widowsbury School did six times, or study at home while you help your dad shell the peas."

"Oh, I do hope you told somebody about Henry!" cried Beatrice, clasping her tiny hands together.

"Tried," said Steffen with a shrug. "Not much use, though. Everybody ignores me."

Adelaide, too, ignored Steffen and instead listened in on the conversation of two teachers across the auditorium.

". . . a terrible feeling about this. This is the third disappearance in three days, you know!"

"Three? I thought it was two! Who's the other one?"

"First there was Elmer Whitley, and then there was Caroline Patterson's boy."

"Oh, I forgot about Elmer. And that poor child! They say his mother hasn't said a word of sense since she turned up ranting and raving in the park yesterday. I always said she was destined for bad luck, living at a twelvey address and all, but she refused to move. . . ."

"I found your librarian's suitcase in the trash."

Adelaide turned and glared at Steffen.

"Wh-what?" she said.

"Yeah," said Steffen, stuffing his kite string back into his bag and exchanging it for a pair of tarnished opera glasses. "That's where I found these. You don't think she'll want them back, do you?"

"That isn't funny, Steffen. We all liked her very much," Beatrice said quietly. "Or don't you know she's gone away?"

"*What* did you say about Miss Delia?" Adelaide asked Steffen again.

Steffen suddenly found himself surrounded, and he wished he hadn't spoken at all.

"You know, you're all kind of scary. Anybody ever tell you that?" he asked.

"All the time," Adelaide hissed.

Steffen gulped. "Hey, I—I—I didn't mean anything by it. Honest! I didn't know she left. I was just wondering why she threw out all her stuff, is all!"

Maggie lurched forward and grabbed him by his shoulders with such force he yelped in surprise.

"Explain!" Adelaide growled.

"Okay! *Okay!*" said Steffen, wincing. "I was looking for old lightbulbs this morning. I wanted to use them for this thing I'm making, and—"

"Get to the point!" Adelaide ordered as Maggie tightened her grip.

"I'm—ow!—I'm getting to it!" said Steffen. "I was looking through your trash cart, and I found a lady's suitcase. It was just like the one I saw with that new librarian. It had a bunch of things in it still!"

"Things like what?" asked Adelaide.

"Clothes and toothpaste and stuff! You know! What *everybody* puts in their suitcases!"

"Did you keep it, Steffen Weller?"

"Ow! No! But it's probably in the garbage still! The trash men don't come until tomorrow morning. Would you tell your friend not to crush me to death?" Steffen complained.

Maggie released him.

"Do you know what this means?" Adelaide asked the others.

"Yes! Er . . . no," said Beatrice.

Adelaide paced. "If Miss Delia quit like Mrs. Merryweather said, she would have taken her things with her, don't you think?" she said.

"But wouldn't she have also taken her things if she'd been fired?" asked Beatrice.

"Exactly!" said Adelaide. "Which leads me to think maybe she didn't even get the chance!"

Steffen, having recovered from the shakedown, was curious now.

"So, you're saying Miss Delia was on the run?" he asked.

"No, stupid," said Maggie.

"I'm saying that maybe she didn't leave at all. *Maybe* she's being held prisoner! Or worse!" said Adelaide.

Beatrice pouted. "But that's what I was trying to say earlier!"

The others were skeptical.

"Think about it!" said Adelaide. "Obviously, Mrs. Merryweather didn't want us to know what really happened. Maybe she threw Miss Delia's suitcase out to hide the evidence! Then there are all these other disappearances. Mrs. Merryweather complained about Elmer Whitley all the time because he was sloppy, and he never brought in enough coal."

"And he swore in front of us!" Beatrice whispered.

"Henry Fernberger's parents are the richest people in town, so you know he's got to be worth some ransom money," Adelaide continued.

"Not to mention he's a royal pain in the neck!" Steffen added.

"Let me see if I understand. You're saying that Mrs. Merryweather kidnapped-or-did-worse to all these people?" said Maggie.

"Possibly!" said Adelaide.

"Even the Patterson kid everybody's talking about?"

"What's to stop her? Maybe she's just all-around evil."

Beatrice, forgetting she wasn't in class, raised her hand. "But Mrs. Merryweather was at school when the little Patterson boy got taken. She had to be because we were outside with Miss Delia then, and that's when Becky told on us."

"Yes, but . . . oh," said Adelaide.

Adelaide remembered the woman wailing in the park the day before. "My son is gone! Have you seen Cornelius? Cornelius, come back!" she had said. *But I ignored that woman,* she thought with a pang of guilt.

"Never mind, then. Just a thought," said Adelaide. "Either way, I think we can safely say that Miss Delia didn't just waltz out of town. You don't travel to a whole new place with all you own in a suitcase just to leave all you own behind. I think it's connected to all these other vanishings somehow, and I'd bet there are clues somewhere in or on that suitcase!"

Beatrice applauded but then stopped upon seeing that no one else shared her enthusiasm.

"What's the big deal about this Miss Delia, anyway?" asked Steffen. "She wasn't here very long, you know. Why do you care where she's gone?"

It was Beatrice who finally answered when the others fell quiet.

"She was the only person in the entire school who was ever nice to us, even a little bit," she said in a voice so small that Steffen wasn't sure whether he actually heard her or if it was the sadness in the girls' faces that answered his question.

Before he could say anything else, the doors to the auditorium creaked open and the senior teachers returned soaking wet, headed by Mrs. Merryweather and her gargantuan umbrella. At once the chatter ended as everyone eagerly awaited news of the latest excitement.

"Ladies of Madame Gertrude's," Mrs. Merryweather began somberly. "I have an unfortunate announcement to make."

She waited an age before she continued.

"As some of you may have heard," she said slowly and gravely, "a student from Rudyard has gone missing. This poor child is Henry Fernberger, whose disappearance I find personally distressing, for the Fernbergers have been dear friends of Madame Gertrude's and of Rudyard School for many years."

"More like their *money's* been a dear friend," Steffen grumbled. "My dad says—"

"Shush! I'm listening to this!" Adelaide whispered.

"It is thought that Henry may have ventured outside of Rudyard School to study independently," Mrs. Merryweather continued.

"Hah!" laughed Steffen.

"He was last seen early this morning," said Mrs. Merryweather. "As some of you may have heard, there have been other disappearances in recent days. So it is out of concern for your safety that I am suspending all day trips—supervised or otherwise—until further notice."

The youngest girls groaned because they had a field trip planned to the nature museum (formerly the Widowsbury Arboretum). The oldest girls groaned because they had plans to watch the boys' rugby game. Everyone else groaned simply because it seemed appropriate for the occasion.

"And it goes without saying," Mrs. Merryweather said, "that no one may have visitors without strict perm—"

She stopped. Her eyes narrowed on a target at the back of the room.

"What is your name, sir?" Mrs. Merryweather bellowed at Steffen. Her booming voice echoed throughout the enormous auditorium and bounced off the rafters.

Steffen looked all around, hoping that, by some chance, he was not actually the only boy present. Realizing his fate, he hung his head and stuttered his reply.

"What are you doing here, Mr. Weller?" spat the headmistress.

"I was running errands for my dad," he mumbled.

"And who is your father, young man? What errands would lead you here?"

Mrs. Merryweather recoiled at his answer. "The *cook's* boy?" she hissed. "Mr. Weller, you have no business among my students, and you will be removed immediately!"

Steffen humbly nodded. He plodded toward the door, but then he paused and turned his head halfway.

"Meet me in front of Rudyard at dawn. I'll bring you the suitcase if you bring me some lightbulbs," he whispered to Adelaide.

Then he ran for the doors before the two teachers coming to escort him could get their hands on his only coat.

"Poor Steffen!" whispered Beatrice.

"Poor nothing. How am I supposed to get outside by dawn?" asked Adelaide.

Mrs. Merryweather left her place at the podium and marched to the back of the room, clearing a path through the other students, who watched the events with mouths hanging rudely open. Beatrice clung to Adelaide's arm as the headmistress drew near.

"I have taken just about all I can stand from you three!" Mrs. Merryweather snarled.

"We didn't do anything!" Adelaide protested.

"Don't talk back to me, girl!" said Mrs. Merryweather, punctuating each word with a jab of her umbrella. "If there are any more disturbances today—any disturbances at all—I will have you and your friends placed in the room upstairs!"

There was a collective gasp among the students. Everybody

knew to which room the headmistress referred. Room 912. The very last door on the ninth floor. It was a place of evil feared above all else. Even Maggie shivered at its mention. Officially, Room 912 was merely a storage place, but everyone at Madame Gertrude's knew of it as the Wailing Room.

Legend told that the Wailing Room had once been a class-room until a substitute teacher was struck in the head with a fallen wall map. She was killed on the spot, they said. Now the room was locked up tight with chains upon chains, and it was reserved only for storage and the very, very worst of students. Students who some-times never came back. For it was also said that the ghost of the dead teacher haunted that room, forever wailing and moaning in anguish until someone very brave could recite all the capital cities of the world. What she did to the students in her domain nobody knew.

This wasn't the sort of story Adelaide normally believed except that she had *heard* the wailing herself on quiet nights when everyone was asleep. It echoed in her dreams and filled her with increasing dread. There was simply no point in arguing with the headmistress any further. Only a fool would dare to test the threat of the Wailing Room.

"Everyone to afternoon classes!" Mrs. Merryweather shouted, and she thrust her soaking umbrella into the hands of a waiting maid.

As the students scattered, Adelaide looked back to Beatrice and Maggie.

"*I'll find a way!*" she mouthed.

*   *   *

73

In the darkness of the raging storm, the lights of Widowsbury twinkled starlike and innocent. Frightened citizens peered from behind each glowing window, wary of new monsters on the outside. Yet none of them knew they were being watched.

Up in the Devil's Thimbles he lurked. A man who was more shadow than man. His yellow eyes gleamed brightly in his hiding place, but he had no fear of being found. He could slip in and out of plain sight as easily as walking through a door. As he did not wish to disturb the delicate progress of his plans, however, he was content to watch from the hills. There he knelt, still as a stone, until a furious wind sent leaves swirling around his wiry frame.

"Shhhh," said the strange man, though he was alone. His voice was soft and light. "I know how anxious you are, but we must take our time."

He gestured to the little town in the valley. "This," he said, "is a dance. We should savor every step. Think of all we have accomplished already, my friend, and here we've only begun!"

As if in answer, the wind shrieked wildly. The stranger smiled a wide and jagged smile and reached into his dark coat. He pulled out a pocket watch made of animal bones and beetle legs and admired its face.

"Yes," he breathed. "It won't be much longer now."

Again, the wind screamed. The stranger softly laughed. Then he rose up on his spindly legs and disappeared into the shadows as if he had never been there at all.

- Chapter Four -
A Letter by Phillip Post

The tempest raged throughout the afternoon and long into the night. Morning, gray and silent though it may have been, was a gift. After storms like yesterday's in a place such as this, one could never be sure if there would be a morning at all. But as someone would soon discover, the trouble was far from over. There was something new in Widowsbury. More specifically, a trail, freshly cut through Henbane Wood.

Nellie Ives discovered the trail while picking nettles in the park at dawn. Against local wisdom, she followed it. Widowsburians had a duty to look out for one another, she reasoned, and she was far too old to be shocked by anything these days. But what Nellie saw at the end of the trail horrified—no—disgusted her.

It was a carousel, brightly painted and gleaming with gold and jewels. Banners and flags hung all around it, flaunting their despicable newness. But there was also a man. A stranger! He stood on a ladder, painting a sign that said OPENING SOON! in letters the color of blood.

"Excuse me! *Excuse* me!" Nellie screeched.

The man on the ladder paused, turned his head halfway, but said nothing. He was tall, and skinny as a rail, Nellie noticed, and dressed all in black like a pallbearer.

She hobbled closer. "What is all this rubbish? Who are you?" she fumed. "Did Mayor Templeton approve this?"

Nellie's breath caught in her throat as the man jumped down from the ladder and crossed over in one giant stride. He curled his arm around her, which she did not like, and bent down so that his teeth were just at her ear.

"Mayor Templeton is still in bed asleep like all good people should be," he said in a voice like molasses. "But now *you* are here, and as you seem to be in charge of things, why, I wouldn't dare continue without your approval! In fact, it's only right, dear lady, that you should be my very first rider!"

The man's breath smelled of rot, and his eyes had a mad look to them. Nellie was terribly uncomfortable, but she found she couldn't look away.

"Well, I don't know," she muttered as the man pushed her toward the ride. This wasn't proper. Not in the least. But the closer she got to the carousel, the less it all seemed to matter. It felt so pleasantly warm in this spot. It was never warm in Widowsbury.

"I suppose I could, just for a little bit," she said. The man smiled. It was an awful grin, far too wide and jagged. But Nellie smiled back all the same as he helped her step onto the platform. She seated herself on a unicorn that sparkled like a million diamonds and watched as the man bowed and stepped back and back and back until she couldn't see him anymore. Now the world was changing around her and showing her such delights! She saw flowers everywhere and in every color. The sun beamed down upon her face. How long had it been since she'd had such fun?

"Yahoooo!" she cheered as the ride began to spin.

By the time the periwinkles wrapped themselves around her and dragged her down with them, Nellie Ives was far beyond hearing.

The tall man dusted off his jacket and returned to his job of sign painting, humming a little to himself as he worked. ALL AGES! he added to the bottom in bright red letters.

Not all good people were asleep at that hour if, in fact, Adelaide Foss was to be considered a good person (and she believed she was). At the moment, she clung to the drainpipe outside the window of the Elevens and Twelves dormitory, six floors up, her toes just barely touching the ledge. In her coat pocket, she carried a pair of lightbulbs she had taken from her bedside lamp. Why the peanut butter boy should need lightbulbs she hadn't a clue. All she could think about was obtaining Miss Delia's suitcase and the clues that might rest inside it.

It had still been dark out when she'd started her escape. The last thing she needed was to be caught sneaking out the window with a pocket full of lightbulbs. It had taken her an hour to get this far. Which wasn't far at all, really, but at least she'd made it outside.

Adelaide hugged the drainpipe with her legs and arms until her knuckles and knees scraped against the outer wall. A moth flitted from her head to the wall, to her hands and around again, tickling her. Adelaide blew at it to make it go away, but even this gave her vertigo and she had to shut her eyes. She felt in between the bricks for a foothold to begin her descent, but some of the grooves were shallower than others. This had all seemed so much easier when she was looking down at it from the safety of the dormitory.

All I have to do is get to the ground. Just one step at a time. Steffen Weller, you'd better wait for me, she thought.

Then she realized with the alarm of someone remembering they'd forgotten the one thing they went to the market for that this was only half of what she'd have to do. She'd also need to get back inside with the suitcase, which meant she'd have to wait for someone to open the door downstairs.

But how would she explain what she was doing outside with the possibly-kidnapped-or-worse librarian's belongings? Adelaide wished she'd thought about it ahead of time. Maggie or Beatrice could have helped her, but then she hadn't wanted to get them involved. More people meant more chances of getting caught, after all. Right about now, Beatrice would probably start crying, and nobody needed that.

Still, Adelaide had gotten this far, so she might as well get on with it, she thought. Perhaps she could claim she'd heard somebody calling for help, and that she found the suitcase sitting outside. Yes. Just sitting outside, and so she thought it might belong to somebody. *Like a missing librarian.* But what if they tried to take the evidence?

Adelaide squeezed nervous sweat out of her eyes and traveled down another few inches. She wondered if Steffen had come out to meet her yet, but she didn't dare look down, and her heart was pounding in her ears.

"All right, Adelaide," she whispered to herself. "You can do this. Keep going."

She made it another foot downward and stopped; she felt something working out of her pockets. *The lightbulbs.* She shifted her position to keep them in place, but it only made them slip out faster. One of them fell to the ground and shattered into glass dust.

She heard someone approaching the window above her. In a panic, Adelaide hurriedly patted the remaining bulb back into her coat pocket with one hand and promptly lost her grip on the drainpipe with the other.

"HELLLLLLLLLP!!!" she screamed. She frantically clawed at the pipe, but her hands were slippery with sweat, and she was losing the battle. The remaining lightbulb slipped away and smashed into nothingness below. So, quite soon, would she.

Until a hand shot out and grabbed Adelaide by her left wrist. The side of the building became a white blur as Adelaide felt herself yanked upward in one swoop. Someone dragged her backward through the window, and then she found herself lying flat on her back on the cold floor. Standing over her was Maggie. Then Miss Patricia. Then everyone else in the Elevens and Twelves.

"That was stupid," said Maggie.

"I know," said Adelaide, dazed and bewildered and incredibly embarrassed. And now her arm hurt. Scarcely had she registered that pain when her ears were filled with the piercing scream of Miss Patricia's whistle.

"Adelaide Foss! To the nurse!" the teacher boomed. "And I don't need to waste my breath telling you where you're spending recess today!"

Moments later, Adelaide and Maggie sat outside the infirmary, waiting for Nurse Özge to report for duty. Miss Patricia had allowed Maggie to go along, seeing as someone had to help Adelaide open doors and things, and Miss Patricia wanted nothing more to do with the matter. Now they sat together in the quiet hallway, looking like a worn-out, mismatched pair of socks.

"Maggie?" said Adelaide.

Did you really throw somebody out a window at your old school? was what she wanted to ask.

"What?" Maggie said.

But Adelaide's courage was gone again.

"I . . . forgot to say thanks before," she mumbled. "So. Um. Thanks."

"Yeah, well, that's the third time I've come to your rescue. First two were a favor. Now you owe me," said Maggie.

"I know," said Adelaide.

"They're calling me Franken-Mag now."

"I heard. I'm sorry, Maggie."

"I thought I was actually going to get through this year without a nickname for once. But no."

"I said I'm sorry, okay?"

"Adelaide! Maggie!" a tiny voice squeaked down the hall. Beatrice raced around the corner, nearly dropping her schoolbooks in the process.

"Oh my gosh! Are you all right? Phillip told me all about it!" she babbled excitedly. "I'm glad I heard it from him because *some* people are saying you were throwing lightbulbs at the boys' school, and others are saying you were trying to climb back in from a night with the . . . !"

Beatrice blushed and stopped before she finished her sentence. *With the wolves.*

"I'm fine," Adelaide grumbled. "I just hurt my arm, is all."

Beatrice sat down in the chair between Maggie and Adelaide, looking confused.

"But I don't understand why you tried to climb out the window. Why didn't you go down the stairs?" she asked.

Adelaide threw her head back and groaned. "Can we stop talking about it? Please?"

She massaged her injured arm. "That Steffen kid is probably out there with Miss Delia's suitcase," she said sadly. "I doubt he'll wait much longer. I think this trail has gone cold."

Maggie picked idly at a stray thread on her uniform.

Beatrice's face fell and then brightened again. "I have an idea!" she said. She opened up her spelling tablet and began to write on it.

"What're you doing?" asked Adelaide.

"I'm writing a letter to Steffen. I'm telling him that we couldn't make it down and could he please hold on to the suitcase for us," said Beatrice as she wrote. She stopped and tapped her chin with her pencil. "Do you think he'd help us if we asked him to?"

Adelaide laughed. "No, I don't think so. We weren't exactly the best of friends yesterday."

"I'm going to ask anyway. *I* think he's nice, and he's our only contact outside. It can't hurt," said Beatrice, and she continued to scribble on her tablet.

"Just how do you think you're going to get a letter to him, anyway?" asked Adelaide.

"Phillip will deliver it for us," said Beatrice. She opened up her pocket.

"It's just this one page, so it shouldn't be too heavy for you," she whispered into it before she patted it closed.

"Marvelous. Phillip Post! Fastest mail mouse in the West," Maggie said with a snort.

Adelaide's heart sank. They couldn't get outside. She'd almost died this morning just for trying. Now their first possible clue as to Miss Delia's disappearance rested in the hands of a weird, smelly boy they might never see again and an imaginary mouse who lived in Beatrice's pocket. This mission was not going at all well.

"All done!" Beatrice chirped, folding up her letter and stuffing it under the cover of her tablet. "I'll send this off as soon as nobody's looking. It's bound to work. I just know it will!"

She hopped up, gathered her books, and skipped gleefully down the hall past an old woman who hobbled toward the infirmary. The woman looked like a witch in a nurse's cap, and she was muttering unintelligible things about mornings *this* and children *that*.

"Hah!" Nurse Özge wheeze-laughed when she saw the girls waiting. "Twisted yer arm throwin' lightbulbs out tha windah, did yeh?"

Adelaide closed her eyes and reminded herself to breathe.

Steffen Weller waited at the front doors of Rudyard School. At his feet was a large black suitcase with flowers on the side, and he was just about to give up on the girl from Madame Gertrude's.

"You try to do a nice thing," he said to himself, not thinking at all about the lightbulbs. Not really.

He had just started to head back inside with the suitcase when he heard a piece of paper sliding across the brick street. He looked down to see if it was anything interesting. It appeared to be a letter. Steffen put the suitcase down on the stoop and bent down to examine the folded-up page.

This was funny.

It was addressed to him.

Steffen looked both ways down the street to see if the writer was around, but there was no one except the milkman farther down the block, and the milkman always got his name wrong. Steffen looked back at the letter and read.

Deer Steffen: Addlade Cuddent make it this morneeng. Will you pleas hold on to the sootcase for us?

Also will you pleas help us fined Miss Delia? Noboddy else will help. Pleas rite yove anser on the back and put it on the ground. Your frend forevar if you help us, Beatrice and Magy and Addlade.

PS: I dont knoe if we can get ennymore lite bolbs for you. Sorey. We tryed.

PPS: Also sorey about Magy she can be growchy sumtimes but she is nice you will sea.

Steffen read the letter again slowly and then once more, until he was sure he understood it. He considered the details: that none of this involved him, he'd only seen the missing librarian once, and there was nothing in it for him anyway.

But.

His father often said that it was best to help people when they ask because help will come back to you trifold, or something like that. And there could be adventure. And secrets! Could there even be something dangerous involved? He hoped so. But then he felt guilty for hoping so, as this involved a real, live human being. Still, it could be interesting, and if it was interesting enough, perhaps he could write a story about it and send it to the adventure magazines.

Steffen read the letter yet again and then wrote his one-word reply on the back, studied the delivery instructions, and dropped the letter on the street. He watched it for a few seconds to see if there were any trained pigeons or other forces at work, but there was nothing of the sort. When the letter didn't move, he gave up and went back inside Rudyard School, dragging the suitcase behind him.

Perhaps it was a gust of air from the closing door that pushed the letter down the street. Maybe a draft from tunnels underneath that sent it traveling along the street in the direction of Mr. Kayso's Cheese Shoppe. It stopped there for a while, and one would expect its journey had ended. But then it turned around and around as if befuddled until it blew back up the street, up the wall of the girls' school, and in through an open window.

LIBRARY

- Chapter Five -

A Horrible Solution

"Adelaide Foss to Mrs. Merryweather's office!" Miss Patricia shouted just as breakfast was about to end.

"Today just isn't your lucky day, is it?" said Maggie.

Adelaide ignored this and headed nervously to the head-mistress's office. She was certain this would be about the incident with the lightbulbs and was rehearsing explanations in her head, but nothing added up. Considering the grave purpose of her mission, she wondered if it might simply be better to accept whatever accusation Mrs. Merryweather made this time. Better that than endanger Miss Delia. But what if Mrs. Merryweather threatened her with the Wailing Room? Adelaide dearly hoped it wouldn't come to that.

As it turned out, Mrs. Merryweather was not interested in the incident with the lightbulbs.

"What is this?" she asked with chilling calm. On the enormous mahogany desk before her lay a large rectangular package wrapped in brown paper. It had a handle on one side, to which there was attached a small tag, fastened with what looked like dental floss. FOR ADDLADE said the tag in large fractured letters. There was no other address that Adelaide could see.

Adelaide sat down slowly on the edge of her chair, hesitant to answer.

"It's a . . . package?" she finally said.

Mrs. Merryweather stood abruptly. "Open it!" she commanded, and she shoved the package toward Adelaide.

Adelaide's palms felt tingly. Her heart was practically in her throat.

"But, Mrs. Merryweather," she began in a wavering voice, "I thought you said it was rude to look at other people's mail. Should you be standing there while I open it? It might confuse me."

She smiled weakly, but this only made Mrs. Merryweather angrier.

"Think this is funny, do you?" the headmistress fumed. "Think it's a laugh to frighten my staff half out of their wits with your unmarked mystery packages? I had to send the mail clerk home for the day, she was so upset! Why not let us all in on the joke, then? Open it, I say!"

"I . . . I'd rather not," Adelaide said, jumping to her feet. "I don't want to be late for First Classes! I'll just take this with me so it won't trouble you anymore. I'm awfully sorry about the—"

"*Sit down!*"

Adelaide promptly fell back into her chair, wide-eyed and trembling. Out in the hall, the bell for First Classes rang. It sounded like the tolling of her own doom. Or, if the package was what she suspected, of Miss Delia's.

"Very well, then," said Mrs. Merryweather. "Since you clearly have something to hide, I shall have to risk my own safety and open it myself."

She produced a frightfully large letter opener from the top drawer of her desk and removed the package's wrapping in three quick slashes. Her eyes narrowed.

"What have we here? A suitcase?" she said. Adelaide felt her heart skip. "Why, this looks remarkably similar to a certain former librarian's suitcase. The very suitcase I ordered thrown out with the rest of her most lazily abandoned items only yesterday! But what . . . *what* was it doing on our doorstep? And in your name, Miss Foss?"

"I . . . um . . . ," Adelaide stalled.

Suddenly Mrs. Merryweather threw open the suitcase and began rifling through it in a most undignified manner.

"No! That doesn't belong to you!" Adelaide cried out, but her protests were hopeless.

"This only confirms my suspicion that you and your cohorts are responsible for Miss Delia's quitting so immediately and so rudely!" Mrs. Merryweather shouted as she flung the suitcase's contents about her desk. "What is in here that interests you so much? Was this what you wanted from that foolish woman? A few articles of clothing and some cheap jewelry?"

"We wanted her to come back!" Adelaide burst out without thinking.

"I beg your pardon?" Mrs. Merryweather roared back. Her face was purple with rage.

"I mean . . . what I mean is . . . I asked the boy from Rudyard to fetch the suitcase for us," Adelaide mumbled, "so that we could hold on to it for Miss Delia in case she ever came back. I didn't think anyone would mind s-s-since it was being thrown away. I'm sorry, Mrs. Merryweather. Really, I am!"

Please believe me! You have to! she wished silently. *It's the most pathetic story I've got!*

Mrs. Merryweather's face returned to its usual colorlessness.

"That woman has left you and your compatriots behind. She doesn't care enough to come back for this or for you," she said coldly. "Between this, the incident in the dormitory, and yesterday's misadventures with the servant boy from Rudyard, I am sorely regretting ever letting you and your friends venture out for recess! Clearly, I was too hasty in my leniency."

She closed the suitcase and pushed it aside, leaving one bony hand resting upon its flowered lid.

"But I have a solution for that, Miss Foss," she said. "You will soon see."

As Adelaide stormed on to her classes, she held back her angry tears and reminded herself that there was still work to be done. This was no time to be wounded by words. But it was difficult to remember the point of it all when her hopes had been dashed yet again.

"Forget about the suitcase," Adelaide grumbled at lunchtime, slamming her tray down beside Beatrice. After the morning's events, a bit of ridicule for sitting with the little kids would hardly be a bother. To her surprise, Maggie was already there.

"What's the matter?" asked Beatrice.

"Steffen delivered it as promised, but Mrs. Merryweather got to it first," Adelaide answered. She slumped down on the bench and grumpily forked her mashed peas. "But it didn't even matter. I watched her search all through it! It was like she'd never seen the inside of it before, and she obviously didn't care if I looked! It was just a dead end for us. And no, there wasn't anything useful in there. It was exactly like Steffen said."

Maggie slurped her milk. "What else did you expect?" she asked.

"I don't know! I just hoped there'd be something in there that was worth the trouble!" said Adelaide. "People think I was out howling at the moon last night. Other people think I was throwing lightbulbs at the boys' school. Mrs. Merryweather actually accused us of driving Miss Delia away, and all for that stupid, stupid suitcase!"

"Yeah, but nobody's calling you Franken-Mag," said Maggie.

"Oh, Maggie, that's awful!" said Beatrice, and she patted Maggie's shoulder.

Adelaide looked around and noticed that several other girls throughout the dining hall were staring at her. It wasn't the usual gawking, either. Barbara Marx, for example, seemed to be shaking her head in pity.

"I have some good news for you," said Beatrice cheerily. She pulled a letter from her pocket and unfolded it. It was the letter she had written to Steffen earlier. On the back was written one word.

"'OK,'" Adelaide read. "OK what?"

"It's from Steffen! It means he's going to help us!" Beatrice explained. "And you thought Phillip couldn't deliver my message."

Adelaide turned around just in time to catch some of the other girls staring again. They quickly looked away. Adelaide couldn't shake the feeling that there was something more to this.

"I've already sent him another message," said Beatrice. "I thought it would be a good idea if he went around town and asked some questions. You know, if anyone saw anything unusual that night."

"Forget Steffen for a minute. Have you two noticed everyone staring at me?" asked Adelaide.

"They're doing it to me, too. More than usual. It's making me very nervous," said Beatrice.

Maggie grunted and twisted her butter knife into the heart of a boiled potato. She, too, had noticed the staring.

Just then Miss Patricia blew her whistle.

"Adelaide Foss! Beatrice Alfred! Maggie Borland! To the library for detention!" she shouted.

"The library?!" Adelaide gasped.

"But who's going to watch us? We haven't got a librarian!" asked Beatrice.

"Right now!" Miss Patricia added.

As the girls marched to their uncertain doom, Steffen Weller worked through his day's round of errands for his father. In one of his coat pockets, he carried another note from Beatrice. This one had managed to get in through the basement window. It said:

Dear Steffen: Thank you! You hav no idia how greatfull we are! Will you ask arownd and sea if any boddy saw Miss Delia? We cannot get ~~out~~ owtside as you knoe.

Thank you agan!

Yore frend,
Beatrice

In his other pocket Steffen carried his father's to-do list, upon which was written a warning to stay on the main streets on account of all the recent bad news. *Well*, he thought. *I guess I can still ask around at the shops.* Though, to be honest, he had no idea what he'd ask them. He remembered very little about Miss Delia from the one time he'd seen her except that she had sort of reddish hair, and she looked a bit frazzled.

The first task had been to pick up a few things from Gorman's Market. He'd asked Mr. Gorman if he'd seen anything strange in recent days, but Mr. Gorman simply said, "Most days!" in a cryptic way, which probably meant nothing because Mr. Gorman had never been quite right since the Big Storm, Steffen's father once said.

After that, he had gone to the sharpening place, where he unloaded a bagful of knives from his squeaky old pull wagon.

"Have you seen a lady with reddish hair? Kind of . . . new?" he had asked the owner, whose name he had never known, for the owner was a retired monk who had not retired his vow of silence. The owner shook his head.

The monk's assistant was more helpful. "You could ask the Smithes. They see everything!" he had suggested. But Steffen hoped he wouldn't have to ask the Smithes.

The cleaners reported nothing when Steffen dropped off the headmaster's table linens. The hardware store had no useful information when Steffen came to pick up canning supplies. And old Mrs. Paisley of Paisley Pot & Pan Retinning thought she may have seen some shadows or something, but Steffen soon realized she didn't know a thing and was merely trying to keep him there for conversation.

"So much for questioning the locals," Steffen said to himself. His adventure story was turning out to be a dull one. "Detective Steffen and the Town Full of People Who Didn't See Anything Strange but Maybe You Could Ask the Smithes." What a bore.

Now Steffen was back on his home street, staring at the bright blue awning of the Smithe & Sons butcher shop with uncertainty. He'd saved this task for last, hoping that something might come up that rendered it unnecessary. Perhaps his father would race over to tell him the school menu had been changed to peanut butter sandwiches all week. Stranger things had happened.

Most of the time, Steffen didn't mind the tasks he had to carry out, but the butcher shop—that one was different. He wasn't sure what bothered him more—the giant slabs of raw meat strung up everywhere or the fact that everyone wore a blood-spattered apron, even the owner's wife, who was always offering him butter toffees.

Steffen studied the list of meats he was supposed to order. Seventy-two veal cutlets. Forty-eight pounds of rump roast. Ninety-six ribs and something called flank. It all sounded perfectly grisly to Steffen, but not the fun kind of grisly he read about in his adventure stories. For one thing, he didn't have a ray gun. Still, he had to do it, and anyway, the sharpening monk's assistant had been right. The Smithes were the nosiest people he knew, and nothing escaped their notice.

The front part of the butcher's shop was always neat and tidy. Everything was white except for a few fake flowers. There was an out-of-date wall calendar that featured photographs of horses, too. But no matter how many scented doilies and silk flowers Mrs. Smithe put out, the place still reeked of raw meat. Steffen ignored this as best he could and stood up on his toes to ring the little silver bell on the counter.

Steffen waited for someone to come to the front and occupied his time with the wall calendar. He noticed that the longer he stared at the horse in the picture, the more it seemed to be watching him right back. He shut one eye and then the other, and then did it again but faster, until it looked like the horse was shaking its head.

"A fan of horses, are you?" said a voice behind him. Steffen yelped in surprise.

"Oh! It's you, Mr. Z!" he laughed.

Mr. Zoethout laughed, too. "Sorry, I didn't mean to scare you, Steffen!"

"How's business?" Steffen asked.

Mr. Zoethout took off his straw hat and smoothed back his unruly brown hair.

"Well, I've had some trouble with the locals. A little vandalism the other day, in fact, but I've seen a few people come around. Nobody—well, not many—can resist a fresh box of chocolate truffles, after all!" he said. Then he craned his neck and shouted toward the back of the shop. "Isn't that right, Mrs. Smithe?"

A little cow-shaped buzzer over the back door went *Mooooo!* as the butcher's wife stepped in from the back of the shop, patting her forehead with a stained washcloth.

"Is that you, Mister Zoethout?" she asked merrily, much to Steffen's surprise.

Mr. Zoethout tipped his hat to her and smiled, causing the butcher's wife to blush.

"Don't you wink your eye at me, young man! I'm old enough to be your mother!" she laughed. When she laughed, her whole body shook.

"My mom would've been jealous of you, Mrs. Smithe," said the candy man, "but I think you've overlooked your best customer!"

Mrs. Smithe seemed confused for a moment, until she finally noticed Steffen.

"Yes, of course! My word! I didn't see you standing there, boy. What can I get for you today?" she asked, but her tone had lost all its joy again, and Steffen had the distinct feeling that he'd interrupted the grown-ups. He hated moments like these because they reminded him that he was just a kid. He didn't say anything when he reached up to hand Mrs. Smithe his father's list. He didn't even wait for her to tell him it would be ready by three o'clock as usual before he shuffled out the door.

Then he remembered something. He wasn't just a kid. He had a case to solve!

"I forgot to ask you something, Mrs. Smithe," he said.

"Yes?" she asked, irritated. Mr. Zoethout, too, seemed a little annoyed, and Steffen was almost too embarrassed to ask his question.

"This might sound strange, but have you seen anything unusual recently? Perhaps in the night?" asked Steffen.

"No, I don't believe so," said Mrs. Smithe.

"Neither have I," said Mr. Zoethout.

Steffen thanked them and began to walk out the door again. What a waste of time this detective work was turning out to be, he thought. No clues. No people of interest. Not anything in it for him. Helping people was all very well and good, but it wasn't very rewarding, he was finding.

"Unless you count going out for a late-night walk as strange!" he heard Mrs. Smithe say to Mr. Zoethout with a girlish giggle.

Steffen turned back.

"Although I think it's stupid more than strange," Mrs. Smithe was saying.

"Go on, please," said Steffen. "I mean, if you don't mind."

Mrs. Smithe looked at him funny.

"The poor thing is new in town, so I imagine she just didn't know any better," she said. "That new librarian from the girls' school, I mean. Herbert saw her night before last. Just walking along in the dark toward the park like she was out for a stroll in any ol' town! I told Herbert he should say something to her, but he doesn't like to get involved."

"How come you didn't say anything?" Steffen asked, and Mrs. Smithe blushed again, looked over at Mr. Zoethout, and blushed even more.

"She *is* new," she huffed. "She may be very nice, but you just never know!"

"What's on your mind, Steffen?" asked Mr. Zoethout.

"Nothing! Never mind!" Steffen said hastily, and he hurried out the door.

Finally, a clue! A big one! Steffen's heart leaped in his chest. The librarian had gone out for a walk, and she'd gone to the park. The Patterson kid disappeared in the park. The handyman from the girls' school—his truck had been found by the park. The only one he wasn't sure about was Henry, but he would bet dollars to donuts (whatever that meant) that Henry had gone to the park as well.

He ran down the sidewalk, the details swishing around in his head like a bowl of stew on a bumpy car ride.

The park. They had gone to the park. He drafted a letter to Beatrice in his head. *Dear Beatrice, I think there's something in the park, and . . .*

He heard footsteps behind him and turned around to see Mr. Zoethout running to catch up to him.

"Steffen! Wait!" Mr. Zoethout called out. "Before you go home, I wanted to ask you about something!"

"Okay," said Steffen.

"I've been working on ways to drum up business," said Mr. Zoethout. He motioned for Steffen to wait while he caught his breath. When he had, he said, "If it works out, I'll be able to open up a real store! But I could use some help getting started, and that's difficult to get in this town. You looking for a job?"

Steffen's first instinct was to shout *Yes!* He'd always wanted a real job. None of the boys at Rudyard had jobs. But if he worked for Mr. Zoethout, who would help his father? And if nobody helped his father, there wouldn't be time for their lessons. His dad would be heartbroken. Steffen's smile faded.

"I would love to, Mr. Z, but . . . I don't know if I could. I've got other responsibilities," he said.

Mr. Zoethout patted him heartily on the back. "I understand," he said. "The position's open anytime you need it. Hey! That reminds me! I brought you something!"

"You did?" asked Steffen. Few people ever brought him anything.

"I've been thinking about your candy problem," said Mr. Zoethout, fishing around in his coat pockets until he found a small paper bag. "Peanut butter gumdrops! I think I've invented a recipe that won't give you a stomach ache."

"Gosh, Mr. Z, you didn't have to . . . ," Steffen began.

"Now, you don't have to eat them all unless you want to. I'd be happy if you just tested one for me," said Mr. Zoethout. "There's got to be other people with the same problem, and I'd love to have something available for everyone!"

"Well . . . all right. If it would help you," said Steffen.

He peered into the bag and selected a piece. Then he chewed it thoughtfully for a few seconds. It really was quite good. But scarcely had he swallowed it when he felt a twinge in his belly. He shook his head.

"No?" said Mr. Zoethout. "Doggone it. Back to the kitchen for me. Thanks for the help again, Steffen, and don't forget my job offer!"

"Sure thing," said Steffen, and he headed back toward home, wishing just for a second that his father had somebody else to run his errands.

Speaking of errands, he remembered he had to tell someone something. Something of interest to the girls across the street. Except he'd completely forgotten what he was remembering.

Adelaide, Maggie, and Beatrice sat in their usual seats in the library and waited for whatever terror was about to befall them now. There had been no announcement of a new librarian. Mrs. Merryweather hated watching them herself. There was always the chance of one of the other teachers taking over the spot. Maybe Miss Patricia. That wouldn't be so bad. All she ever did was yell a lot and blow her whistle. But Adelaide had begun to itch all over. Every fiber of her being knew that something bad was about to happen.

"What do you suppose would happen if we just walked out? Right now?" Adelaide asked.

Beatrice blanched. "We couldn't! We'd be in such trouble!"

"It's too late, anyway. I can already hear someone coming," Adelaide grumbled.

Beatrice bent down to the floor and cupped her hands as if catching something, which she lifted to her ear. "Hush, everyone! Phillip says Mrs. Merryweather is right outside the door!" she reported. "He says she has someone with her! It's Becky!"

Maggie was about to say something rude when the library door swung open. Mrs. Merryweather marched inside, the taffeta of her gown swishing as she moved. Behind her, just as Beatrice foretold, was the infamous Becky Buschard.

"You really have to stop doing that, Beatrice. It's weird," Adelaide whispered with a shudder.

"Girls," said Mrs. Merryweather, "meet your new detention teacher."

Becky curtsied. Adelaide felt her heart drop from her chest. *No. It wasn't possible!*

"I simply cannot spare any other teachers, and they were not hired to watch you three bring shame upon our great institution!"

said Mrs. Merryweather. "Miss Buschard has graciously offered her leisure time to watch the three of you until a new librarian can be found. For her efforts, she will receive extra credit, which will be applied to all her final exams this year. Miss Buschard will no doubt graduate with honors when she leaves us in four years. You three would do well to learn by her example!"

Maggie snorted and then coughed to disguise it. Becky glared at her with fury in her eyes, but her sneering smile never left her lips.

"If those three give you any difficulties, report them to me," said Mrs. Merryweather. She looked at them. "One toe over the line will send them directly upstairs!"

With that, she left them alone with the most evil fourteen-year-old in recorded history.

As soon as the library door was closed, Becky reached across the desk behind her and slid a yardstick from the top of it. It made a slithering sound like a snake's belly as she dragged it slowly and deliberately across the surface.

"Oh, we're going to be *such* friends," she said, and she cackled, slapping one palm with the end of the yardstick. "In fact, we're going to be such good friends that you'll do whatever I say! Won't you?"

"I don't have to do anything you say!" Adelaide blurted, which she instantly regretted.

"Careful, Miss Foss," said Becky. "I have only to say the word, and you'll be locked up in Room 912 for weeks. In fact, I just might say the word whether you've done anything or not! Why? Because

I don't like you. Any of you. So, you'd better work hard to *make* me like you. Understood?"

No one said anything.

"Answer me!" Becky ordered.

"Yes, Becky," Beatrice said quietly.

"'Yes, Miss Buschard,' you mean."

"Whatever you want, Miss *Butchered*," Maggie muttered.

Becky strolled casually to Maggie's seat. *Whack!* went the yardstick on the table, but Maggie didn't flinch.

"You'd better respect me or you'll pay for it, and so will your friends," Becky threatened. Then she straightened and moved to the front of the library.

"All right, ladies. You will now stand!"

The girls reluctantly obeyed, much to Becky's delight. She paced back and forth, eyeing the girls like a tiger hunts its prey.

"Up on the tables!" she commanded.

"What?!" said Adelaide.

"You heard me," said Becky. "Climb up onto the tables and stand! And don't look at each other like that. You're plotting something, and I'm not going to allow that. Keep your eyes only on me!"

The girls started to rise.

"Actually . . . scratch that," said Becky.

They sat again.

"Adelaide, I want you to come over and stand on my desk."

"You don't have a desk," said Adelaide.

"When I'm in here, *this* is my desk!" Becky shouted, pointing at the vacant librarian desk. "Now get over here and climb up on it, or all three of you are going to the Wailing Room if I have to take you there myself!"

Adelaide, humiliated, complied.

"Now," Becky said to Adelaide with a cruel grin, "howl."

Adelaide was speechless.

"Do it or you know where you're going!" Becky screeched.

"N-no," said Adelaide, but Becky showed no sign of relenting.

Beatrice began to cry. Maggie rose abruptly from her chair, but Adelaide held up her hand.

"No, it's—it's okay," she said. "I'll do it."

"I'm losing patience," said Becky.

Tears spilled down Adelaide's cheeks, and she didn't bother to hide them. She took a deep breath and then another and then she howled just like a wolf.

"Excellent! Now we're ready for some real fun," Becky cackled.

The next few days were an endless stream of tortures. All pure delight for Becky Buschard. They danced like clowns if she wanted them to. They did her homework. She made them watch while she rehearsed for the school play, and sometimes they had to act as her stage props. Of all the days they had spent at Madame Gertrude's School for Girls, these were by far the worst.

One afternoon Maggie saw Steffen walking down the hallway, struggling with a bag of potatoes. He looked like he was trying to remember something that was just on the tip of his tongue.

"Steffen!" she yelled. He turned around and dropped his potatoes.

"Have you found anything out yet?" Maggie asked him.

"Yes. I think so. I mean, I did. I don't know," he answered. He collected his potatoes.

"What do you mean you don't know?"

"I mean . . . I forgot," he said. "I don't know how, but I forgot. It was important, though. It had something to do with your Miss Delia."

"How could you forget something like that?" Maggie snapped. "Did someone see her? Did anyone hear something about her? Anything?"

"I told you! I tried to remember, but I can't! As soon as I do, I promise I'll tell you!" Steffen insisted. He finished stuffing potatoes back into his bag, but Maggie grabbed his wrist before he could stand.

"You'd better," she said, "and now I have to ask your help with something else."

Her voice was low. Threatening. She wasn't asking him anything. She was *telling* him. Steffen was afraid.

"I hear you invent things," said Maggie.

"Y-yeah?" Steffen gulped.

"Good," said Maggie, "because we need an invention to drive off a bully."

"Look, I don't want to get into any trouble," said Steffen. "I've got bully problems of my own!"

Maggie looked back and saw that Miss Patricia was eyeing them suspiciously.

"I don't have time to explain," she whispered. "Just wait for a note from me. You got that?"

"Uh . . . !"

Miss Patricia's sizable figure drew near, and Maggie released Steffen. She pantomimed the writing of a letter, then hurried down the hall and was gone.

Steffen looked ahead, then at his bag of potatoes, then up at the ceiling.

"What've I gotten myself into?" he asked aloud. Then he lumbered down the stairs with his potatoes, struggling and failing to recall what it was he'd wanted to tell the girls in the first place.

For the unlucky three, the tortures continued. There was even a day Becky made them march down the hall with sandwich-board signs that said things like I AM A CIRCUS FREAK and ASK ME ABOUT RATS. There was no escape from Becky and no defense against her cruelty, for she carried the worst weapon of all: Mrs. Merryweather's approval. With the headmistress's blessings, she could send them to the Wailing Room on a whim if she liked. The threat was always there, and just in case they doubted the seriousness of that threat, she told them terrifying new tales. Accounts of students who'd been sent to 912, never to return. Stories of screams in the night.

It seemed the torture would never end. Until Maggie divulged her plan.

"I have an idea. Been working on it for a couple of days," she mumbled at lunch one day. She slipped a few notes out from under her lunch tray. One was for Adelaide. One was for Beatrice, and the other was for Beatrice to send to Steffen, however it was she managed to do it. Then Maggie abruptly left. Soon after came the sound of a food tray crashing, startled shouts, and Miss Patricia's whistle.

"She's distracting the teachers so we won't get caught with these. Hurry!" Adelaide whispered.

She eagerly read her note and then the one intended for Steffen.

"It's brilliant!" she murmured.

Beatrice was less enthusiastic.

"I'm not sure if they'll do it," she said, "but if it's our only choice . . . all right. I'll talk to them."

Caroline Patterson stood alone on a path in the woods, shaking from head to toe. She had never seen this path before.

"Known is good, new is bad . . . ," she recited fearfully. She did not want to go any farther, but she knew she had to. Her son was in there. She had heard him!

"Cornelius?" she shouted. "Cornelius, are you there?"

"Mama!" the little boy called again, but she could not tell where the sound was coming from.

"Mama's here, Cornelius! Where are you?" she called back.

A gust of wind made knots of Mrs. Patterson's graying hair, and it carried with it the song of Cornelius's playful giggle. *If he's been hiding from me all this time, he'll have no more chocolate bars for a year!*

Mrs. Patterson thought, though she'd have given every chocolate bar in the world to find him safe and sound. She had even brought a few with her, for she knew how he adored them.

"Over here, Mama!" said the voice.

This time the voice was clear. So clear she could have found him in the dark.

"Stay where you are! I'm coming!" Mrs. Patterson cried.

She ran hard and fast down the mysterious pathway, never minding the little stones that tumbled into her shoes. Mrs. Patterson ran and ran until she came upon a most unusual sight. But she quickly forgot that sight.

"There you are!" she exclaimed, and she rushed to embrace her lost little boy.

Only there wasn't anyone else. There was only Mrs. Patterson alone in the woods on a carousel.

- CHAPTER SIX -

Something Is Hungry

A t last, the night everyone in town awaited all year had come. The annual play at Madame Gertrude's was as close to genuine theater as Widowsbury ever got, and everyone who was anyone attended. They were afraid not to, for any break in routine might look suspicious, particularly in these darkening times.

This year's play was a medley of famous scenes from Shakespearean plays like *Julius Caesar* and *Antony and Cleopatra*. In the dressing room, the actresses practiced and primped in front of mirrors while Mrs. Merryweather made sure that everyone looked as perfect as possible. The reigning queen of the evening was Becky, who was to star in three separate scenes from *Romeo and Juliet*. And she made sure that everyone knew her place.

"Out of my way!" she snapped, pushing girls away from the biggest mirror in the dressing room to meek replies of "Sorry, Becky!" and "My fault, Becky!"

"Do you need a moment alone?" Mrs. Merryweather asked her star performer.

Becky smiled angelically. "Only if it's no trouble!" she said sweetly. "I wouldn't want to inconvenience the rest of the cast! My parts aren't so important."

"Nonsense!" said Mrs. Merryweather. "You are the star of the play! You must have as much time as you need!"

Mrs. Merryweather immediately ordered everyone else backstage. She did not see the feet sticking out from under the props left in the hall.

"How long do you think we've got until someone asks where we are?" whispered a pine tree.

"I doubt anyone cares so long as we're out of sight," said a cactus.

Between them, the moon sneezed.

Adelaide, Maggie, and Steffen freed themselves from their hiding places and checked once more to make sure nobody else was around.

"Can I come out now?" asked a small voice from a hollow boulder.

Maggie lifted up the rock for Beatrice.

"Are you sure you can handle this?" Adelaide whispered.

Beatrice bit her lip and nodded quickly.

"Good," said Adelaide. "Thank you for coming, Steffen. Have you got everything ready?"

Steffen patted his knapsack and gave a thumbs-up sign.

Adelaide carefully pushed open the back door to the dressing room just wide enough for Beatrice and Steffen to slip through.

Steffen looked back at Maggie and nodded. Maggie nodded, too, her arms laden with folding chairs.

"O Romeo, Romeo!" Becky recited before the mirror. "Wherefore art thou Romeo?"

She dotted her lips with scarlet lipstick despite the fact that proper ladies probably didn't wear such a thing in Juliet's day.

"*Where*fore art thou? Where*fore* art *thou?*" she rehearsed.

Suddenly the dressing-room door slammed shut, and the lights flickered out like dying flames.

Becky jumped up from her stool and squinted in the darkness. "Who's there? Turn the lights back on! I mean it!" she said.

On the vanity table, her script flew open. Its pages turned of their own accord.

"What's going on?" Becky asked. "Is someone playing a joke on me?"

Splink!

Becky spun around.

Splink! Splink! Crash! Splink! One by one, all the lightbulbs around the mirror exploded.

She stumbled backward, shielding her face with her arms. "Petronella, if this is your idea, you'd better stop or you *will* regret it!" she threatened.

"It's not Petronella," said a small voice. Becky knew that voice. It was one of the kids she watched during detention, wasn't it?

There was a small flicker of light and then a candle bloomed to life. Except no one was holding the candle. In the glow of its floating light, she saw the face of her visitor. Yes. It *was* one of the scary kids. The littlest one, who was always hanging around the werewolf girl. What was her name again? *Beatrice.*

"What are you doing in here, Beatrice? You're supposed to be sitting in the audience right now, waiting for me to perform!" Becky shouted.

"But you *are* performing," said Beatrice. There was a crackle of paper, as if she was reading a script herself. In the glow of the floating candle, Beatrice's eyes were like two black stones, and her pale little cheeks looked sunken and ghostly.

Becky glanced up at the ceiling and all around the candle.

"I know how you're doing that. You've got strings. I can see them," she said.

"Never mind the candle," said Beatrice.

Someone pulled Becky's tiara from her head and hurled it across the room, where it made a tiny *tink!* as it hit the floor.

"Who did that?" Becky shrieked. "Who else have you got in here, you little brat? Is it one of your imaginary friends or somebody breathing?"

"There's no one," said Beatrice. Her voice sounded so sad, which made it all the more frightening. She took a step closer. Becky fumbled blindly for something with which to protect herself, knocking her script off the table and startling herself even more.

"Listen to me, you little freak!" she yelled, brandishing a hairbrush. "I've got to be onstage in ten minutes! Whatever it is you want, you'd better spit it out now or I'll make you write until your hands bleed tomorrow!"

Beatrice heaved a heavy, world-weary sigh. "Please don't do that," she said. "I'm here to give you a message. They told me you wouldn't listen. I hoped ever so much they'd be wrong."

As Becky ran toward the side door, a small footstool moved all by itself to block her path. When she tried to kick it out of the way, something pushed her wig down on her forehead. She felt things—hundreds of tiny things like pins and needles—poking at her all over. She tried to open the door but something on the other side was stopping it from budging, and when she ran toward the back door, her path was blocked by several folding screens, which raced across the floor and closed around her.

"*Stop it! Let me out!*" she screamed. She kicked down the screens, but it only got worse.

Small pieces of costume wear sprang at her from all sides. Her lipstick flew through the air and dotted her arms and cheeks with red smudges. And someone was pulling at her real hair.

"Ow, ow, ow, ow! Stop it! Please! Somebody help me!" she cried as she flailed frantically at her invisible attackers.

"Until you listen to me, I'm afraid it won't stop," said Beatrice.

Becky dropped to the floor and curled up in a ball, her arms over her head, which was being pelted with hair rollers.

"What do you want?" she sobbed.

Beatrice cleared her throat, and Becky again heard the crinkle of paper.

"My message is," Beatrice said as if reading, "leave us alone. You will never hurt us again. You will not make us wear mean signs and walk around the school until everybody laughs at us. You won't ever threaten us with the Wailing Room again. In fact, you should probably go back to recess from now on and forget about your extra credit. You're a terrible person, Rebecca Buschard, and the only people who like you are just pretending. Go away and never bother us again."

"All riiiiiiight!" Becky wailed pitifully.

"And you won't say a word about this to Mrs. Merryweather, either. Do you promise?"

"Yes, I promise! Make it stop!"

Just as suddenly as it had begun, the attack ceased. The candlelight went out. The poking and pulling stopped. The costumes and makeup fell to the floor from midair, as dead as such things ought to be.

Becky was afraid to look up again. She could hear muffled voices and the sound of heavy objects scraping the floor outside. Then the door finally opened. She felt a pair of cold hands on her arms, and she screamed.

"Becky! What on earth is the matter? Who stacked up all these chairs outside?! You've got to go onstage!" said Mrs. Merryweather.

"Is she gone?" asked Becky.

"Is who gone? What . . . what have you done to yourself?" asked Mrs. Merryweather. She covered her mouth with one hand, horrified.

Becky wiped her hand across her nose, inadvertently smearing lipstick all over her face. "I have to go onstage!" she exclaimed, her eyes wide and crazy. "They're waiting for me! They're *waiting* for me!"

She fled the dressing room and ran backstage, followed by an extremely unhappy Mrs. Merryweather.

Beatrice slipped out the back door, where Adelaide and Maggie waited, almost bursting with their laughter.

"What?" Beatrice asked sullenly.

"What do you mean *what?*" said Adelaide. "That was fantastic! You should have seen her come running out of there! What a mess! What a hilarious mess! Where's Steffen? I've got to congratulate him on his puppetry."

But Beatrice wasn't laughing. "I don't think it's hilarious at all," she said.

"What's the matter with you?" asked Adelaide. "It was brilliant! You must have been really convincing. She was terrified! I only wish I could've seen it!"

Beatrice shook her head. "I don't think we ought to have done it. It wasn't right. I don't like to ask my friends to hurt people," she said.

"Ridiculous," Maggie snorted. "Your friends are ghost rodents. If they were capable of doing anything, they probably enjoyed it."

"Don't say that, Maggie! They're not like that!" Beatrice cried.

"Come on, Beatrice," said Adelaide. "Becky would've done the same to us given the chance. You know she would!"

"Yes. She would. And now we're just like her!" Beatrice sniffled, and she ran away to the auditorium.

Steffen emerged from the dressing room, wide-eyed and pale.

"Steffen. That was amazing. Whatever you did in there, it really worked!" Adelaide gushed, but Steffen was shivering.

"All I did was the candle," he said. His voice sounded far away, and his hands were trembling.

"Huh?" said Maggie.

"What's wrong with you?" asked Adelaide.

"Don't leave me alone with Beatrice ever again. Actually, don't ask me to do any favors for you at all," he said. "I . . . I gotta go home."

He waved halfheartedly and wandered zombie-like down the hall.

"Fine!" Adelaide called out. "See if we do any favors for *you*!"

But Steffen was already gone.

"Well," said Adelaide after an uncomfortable silence, "I guess we should head back, then. If we're not there, someone might figure it all out."

Maggie shrugged, and they went down to the auditorium, where they ducked into the back row beside Beatrice just as the curtain rose. The music, courtesy of the town marching band, began. The stage lights brightened, and there stood the great Becky Buschard, shaking like a leaf. Her wig was all frizzy and lopsided. Makeup was smeared over her arms and face. Her eyes were wide and red. The audience, confused at first, decided this must be the comedy part of the show, and everyone laughed.

"Romeo, Romeo," Becky said with a faltering voice, all but

drowned out by the audience's increasing guffaws. "Wherefore . . . art . . ."

She didn't even finish her first line before she collapsed in tears.

Beatrice stared into her lap, ashamed of herself. Adelaide and Maggie looked at the walls, the ceiling, the floor—anywhere but the stage. This wasn't quite as entertaining as they'd thought it would be. It was awful, actually. Becky, the towering bully—the evil princess of Madame Gertrude's—had been brought to shambles right before their eyes. All satisfaction they felt was immediately replaced by guilt. *I did that to somebody,* Adelaide thought with shame.

The curtain promptly fell again, and two small girls dressed as fairies twirled about on the stage to keep the audience from suspecting the show had not gone as planned. Adelaide heard rustling behind her and bristled as someone leaned close.

"I have to congratulate you ladies on your performance this evening," said a man's voice. She had heard the speaker only once before, but she remembered him clearly. She didn't dare turn around lest Mr. Zoethout see her guilt, but she could hear the laughter in his voice. She looked over at Maggie, who had gone white as a sheet. If they'd been caught, the consequences could have been horrible.

"I—I—I'm not sure what you mean," Adelaide said, but Mr. Zoethout just laughed under his breath.

"You don't have to be scared of me," he said. "Actually, I wish I'd thought of something similar when I was your age. If you want to talk about it sometime, you know where to find me."

Adelaide turned around in her seat just in time to see Mr. Zoethout tip his hat and slip out of the auditorium.

"He isn't going to tell on us, is he?" Beatrice whispered.

"Somehow, I don't think he will," said Adelaide. Her eyes narrowed. "But for some reason, that worries me even more."

The Dread continued into the next day without any sign of lifting. There was talk of strange sounds in the night, and of people behaving strangely. Everyone suspected everyone of something, and the recent vanishings were of no comfort. To make matters worse, the ladies of the Widowsbury Widows' Bureau had been badgering Mayor Templeton all morning, demanding answers as to the whereabouts of their leader, Nellie Ives.

But down at Madame Gertrude's, it was recess time as usual. Becky bowed out of her detention duty the day after her devastating performance, citing an allergy to moldy books. This left Adelaide, Beatrice, and Maggie quite in the way again and Mrs. Merryweather with a difficult decision to make. They couldn't be free at recess. They certainly couldn't be left alone inside. There was only one obvious solution.

"I think we're going to get the Wall," said Adelaide to Beatrice and Maggie.

Miss Patricia blew her whistle and unrolled a crumpled sheet of paper.

"Petronella Clark! To the Wall!"

A short, freckle-faced girl with crooked teeth dropped her jump rope, whined, and stomped to her place against the white brick school wall.

"Marigold Watts!"

"But . . . !" the girl called Marigold protested in vain.

"To the Wall!" Miss Patricia ordered. "Beatrice Alfred! Adelaide Foss! Maggie Borland!"

"I knew it," Adelaide muttered.

"To the Wall!"

The Wall was like prison. While detention was the place to keep disagreeable people out of sight, the Wall was reserved for the unquestionably bad, and it was the last step before the Wailing Room. Few students ever stayed against the Wall for more than a day. It had a way of breaking a person down.

Adelaide sat on the ground and hugged her knees to her chest. The sharp edges of the bricks poked her in the back, and she wondered how many offenders had dug their fingers into the grooves of the mortar. She looked down and saw that someone had scratched some words into the concrete with a chalky piece of gravel: THE END IS THE WALL IS THE END. JUNIPER S. Adelaide didn't know of any Junipers at Madame Gertrude's. Either this was written a long time ago or . . . she didn't like to think about that.

She glanced over at the others. Petronella Clark was on the Wall for leaving rusty thumbtacks on a teacher's chair. The incident landed the mortified teacher in the infirmary for the rest of the day. Marigold Watts was there for getting into fights again. She regularly brawled for the pure joy of it despite the fact that she regularly lost.

She returned Adelaide's gaze with a dirty look, which looked silly, considering one of her eyes was swollen shut.

"What are you looking at, Fido?" she snapped.

"That's not her name. It's Adelaide! Don't you forget it!" said Beatrice.

"Shut up, Crazy, or do you want to get into it with me, too?" Marigold spat. She leaned over to say something equally menacing to Maggie but stopped short. Maggie had picked a rock up off the ground and, without the slightest bit of effort, crumbled it into fine dust with one hand. Now she calmly looked Marigold dead in the eye. The other girl gulped and kept to herself after that.

"I don't belong here. I'm not a criminal!" Beatrice sniffed.

"Look on the bright side, it's bound to be better than the library," said Adelaide.

Maggie blew the rock dust into the air and wiped her hands on her knees.

"You're new to the Wall, obviously," she muttered. Maggie was a three-time Wall veteran herself. Mostly for defending herself against Marigold Watts.

Across the playground, a group of girls huddled together, laughing and pointing at the Wall. And at the center of this huddle was Becky.

"What is she up to now?" Adelaide asked. "I thought we . . . you know."

"Apparently it didn't stick," said Maggie.

Whatever Becky was telling her friends, it probably wasn't

flattering, but Adelaide couldn't bring herself to listen. She closed her eyes and attempted her sailing-ship daydream again, but the bricks in her back made this exceedingly difficult. And now some-one was poking her left shoulder.

"Is it true what they've been saying?" asked Petronella. She had the scabby nostrils of someone who picks her nose a lot.

"I don't know what they're saying, and I don't want to," Adelaide answered.

Petronella wiped her nose with her hand and scooted closer.

"Well, *I* heard it from someone who's friends with Becky that the reason Becky isn't watching you in detention anymore is because, um, because you gave her fleas."

"What?!" said Adelaide. "That's ridiculous!"

"That's just what I heard," said Petronella, "and she also says you bit her and gave her werewolf disease, and she had to go to the hospital to get amputized—"

"I think you mean immunized," Beatrice interrupted, which got her a jab in the rib cage from Maggie.

Petronella gleefully continued. "And I heard it from my cousin that Maggie held Becky down and threatened to beat her up like she did the teacher from her old school—"

"Oh! Did I now?" Maggie snorted.

"And also Beatrice's mother died in a insane asylum 'cuz she thought she saw ghosts all the time, and every time Beatrice cries, her mom's ghost comes out and attacks people," Petronella finished with a boogery sniff.

"It isn't true!" Beatrice insisted. "My mom's not dead! She sent me a postcard from a mortuary in California just the other day! Adelaide! Maggie! Tell them it isn't true!"

Maggie shook her head and spat in the dirt. Adelaide burst out laughing.

"Werewolf disease?!" she laughed, a little too loudly. "Is that really the best she's got? Werewolf disease?! That's the dumbest thing I've ever heard!"

"The Wall is not for talking!" Miss Patricia shouted before blowing her whistle again for good measure. But then a skirmish at the far end of the playground distracted her, and she was gone once more.

"*Werewolf disease,*" Adelaide harrumphed.

By now they had an audience. At least twenty other girls had gathered in front of the Wall, giggling as if they could just burst.

"Ready?" said one of them. They began to sing.

"*Scar-y chil-dren! Scar-y chil-dren! Where are they? Where are they?*" they sang to the tune of "Frère Jacques."

"*You can't run from Maggie! Adelaide will smell thee! Beatrice cries! Then you die!!*"

Adelaide's jaw tightened. Her nostrils flared.

"Uh oh," Beatrice whispered.

Adelaide jumped to her feet and screamed. It seemed the scream would go on forever. Even Miss Patricia was startled.

"Leave us alone!" Adelaide shouted. "Leave us alone right now, or I'll bite every one of you and give *you* werewolf disease, too!"

The singing girls weren't singing anymore. A flash in Adelaide's eyes told them now would be an excellent time to run, and run fast. Miss Patricia, on the other hand, leaped back into action, charging across the playground like a big, square warship.

"What did I tell you?" she roared. "No talking on the Wall!"

Naturally, the whistle followed.

Adelaide sat down and cried, and she didn't care who knew it. It wasn't fair. It just wasn't fair! She hadn't done anything to anyone. If she was so bad, why would Mrs. Merryweather have left them in the care of another student, anyway? Becky had only gotten what she deserved, after all. Except it didn't work. It just made her even more evil, and now Becky stood at the back of the playground, grinning with cold satisfaction while Adelaide was humiliated even more.

Beatrice waited for Miss Patricia to turn away and gently patted Adelaide's back.

"Don't be sad, Adelaide," she said softly. "It'll be all right. But we have to behave. Don't you see? If we disobey, they'll put us in the Wailing Room. It's the only thing they haven't done to us yet. How will we find Miss Delia, then?"

Adelaide pushed Beatrice away and cried even harder.

"I don't care about Miss Delia anymore. She would've turned out bad anyway," she wept. "I just want to go away from here! Mom and Dad said they put me here for my own benefit, but it's a lie. They want to get away from me! They hate me! They must! If they loved me, they wouldn't have left me here! Sometimes I wish all the awful people in the world would just die and leave us alone!"

"Don't, Adelaide! Don't ever say that!" Beatrice warned. "I've seen what can happen when mean people die! Sometimes their spirits come back, and they're terrible, soulless, awful things! Oh, I wouldn't wish it on anybody. I'd much rather everybody find something that makes them happy so they'll forget to bother us."

She traced a flower in the dirt with her finger.

"But," she said, "I don't understand where Becky would get those ideas about my mother. Unless she means my birth mother. I never knew her. I was always told she moved to Australia and married a man named Gary."

"Beatrice, now is not the time," Maggie chided in a surprisingly gentle voice.

The rest of recess was spent in silence.

Beatrice awoke that night to the sound of frightened squeaks.

"Phillip?" she whispered, but Phillip was not on her pillow where he usually slept. He wasn't under her bed where he liked to play, and he wasn't nesting in her shoes.

Careful not to wake the others, Beatrice crept from her bed and searched.

"Phillip? Where are you?"

She checked the closet in case he was hiding in a pocket, then she stood on tiptoe and felt along the dusty windowsill. No sign of her ghostly pet. She noticed the temperature in the room had dropped to an alarming chill. An Other Ghost.

"Phillip, please come back," Beatrice whimpered.

Mice and squirrels and even cat spirits were all too innocent to affect the temperature, but the Other Ghosts were quite another thing. When people, especially bad people, passed away and returned as ghosts, there was very little left of their former selves. There were only bits and pieces of whatever horror had made them what they were. They were empty inside, and the place where their souls had been sucked all warmth out like a vacuum.

She heard the skitter of teeny paws and saw a little half-transparent grayness disappear through the wall into the washroom.

"Phillip!" she breathed with relief, and she took off after him.

Beatrice found Phillip perched way up high on the sill of the washroom's tiny square window. But he didn't jump down to her as he normally did. Instead, he squealed and vanished into thin air.

A cold whisper raced through the washroom, rustling all the bath curtains, but the window was closed. *Slam!* And now the door was, too. Beatrice stood alone, bathed in moonlight in the center of the pearl white room. She shuddered with cold and fear and hugged herself tightly.

"Phillip . . . ," she quietly cried. The room was beginning to smell like moldy peaches. The odor filled her nostrils and made her feel sick, but she didn't dare move.

There was silence, and then—for just a moment—Beatrice felt warm again. The Other Ghost had left before it appeared. Until the temperature plunged again, and up from a floor drain rose a pale pink vapor.

"Oh no. No, please!" Beatrice squeaked.

The vapor took the shape of a girl. An older girl in a carnation pink dress. Her lips were as gray as her skin, and her hair was brownish and matted with slime. She had only whites for eyes. They always did. She moved her mouth to speak even though no sound came from her throat. They always did that, too.

Beatrice backed toward the door.

"Please. I just want to go back to bed. I don't want to talk to you!" she pleaded.

She spun around, threw open the door, and fled the washroom, but the ghost girl followed her. This they almost never did.

"Leave me alone! Leave me alone! Leave me alone!!" Beatrice cried. She didn't care if she woke anyone up now. But the ghost girl was even closer, and she kept moving her lips in that horrible, silent way.

Beatrice ran from the Nines and Tens dormitory to the hallway. She hoped with all hope that this ghost simply haunted the sleeping quarters and not the whole floor.

Surely, she only haunted this floor, and not the whole west wing!

Surely, it was just this wing and not the entire school!

Beatrice ran and ran until she found herself in the boiler room of the east wing. It was completely dark there. *Good*, she thought. The ghosts who visited in any kind of light usually didn't venture into the shadows and vice versa. Beatrice didn't know why this was—only that it was or, at least, had been as far as she knew.

She moved through the darkness, and when her eyes adjusted, she searched for even darker places, at last deciding on a space between two giant tanks. Normally, the hiss of gas and the roar of the furnace frightened her, but the sounds were comforting now,

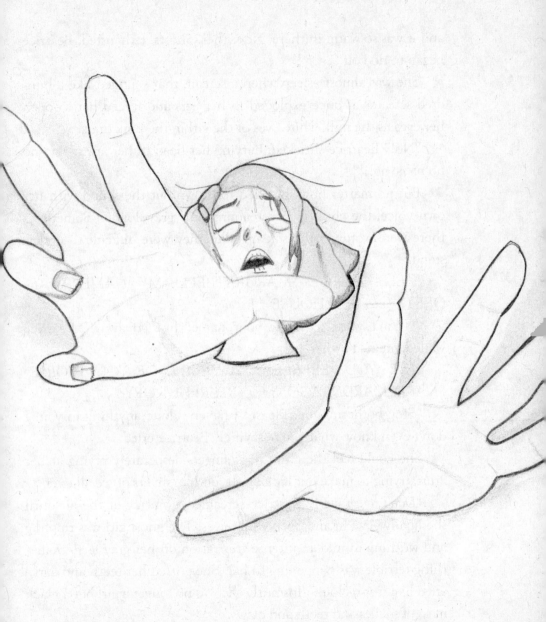

and it was so warm in there. No Other Ghosts. Exhausted, Beatrice began to nod off.

She was almost asleep when a scream that sounded like a hundred screams at once exploded in her ears and forced her to open her eyes to the milk white eyes of the girl in the pink dress.

"No!" Beatrice shrieked, burying her head in her arms. "No no no *no no no*!!!"

But no matter how she tried to drown out the sound with her own voice, the ghost girl's screaming only grew louder. Sometimes there were words in the screams, but they were difficult to understand.

"BELL! HOUSE! MARGRETBELL! MY NAME! MARGRET . . . ! BELLHOUSE . . . !"

"I don't want to know your name! Just go away!" Beatrice wailed, muffled by her arms.

"EAT YOU! EEEEEEAT YOU! ALL OF YOU! HORSESNAKELIZARDDRAGONMONSTER! HUNGRY!"

"Stop bothering me! Please! I haven't done anything to you! I don't even know what you're saying!" Beatrice cried.

She could feel the ghost girl's fingers desperately prying at her arms, trying to make her look up. It felt like slivers of ice all over.

"Don't touch me!!" Beatrice screamed, swatting at the air until she finally gave in and opened her eyes. The ghost girl was rippling and writhing in midair, intense frustration on her gray face. Something terrible was happening to her. She gritted her teeth and darkened like storm clouds. Instantly she was no longer a girl but a black mass of snakes and teeth and claws.

Beatrice screamed and ran from the boiler room, but the ghost girl's voice was inside her head now, whispering dreadful messages where Beatrice could not escape them.

An awful ruckus jarred Adelaide from her sleep.

"Adelaide! Maggie!" someone was screaming.

"Huh?" she said sleepily. She looked around the room and saw that most of her dorm mates were also sitting up in bed, equally confused.

"Adelaide!"

It was Beatrice, restrained by Miss Patricia and another grumpy teacher, both in nightgowns.

"What are you doing up here? You'll wake up the entire school!" Miss Patricia shouted as she struggled to hold on to the hysterical girl.

"Beatrice?" Adelaide whispered. She had never seen Beatrice behave this way before, and it frightened her.

"No! Listen to me!" Beatrice wailed as Miss Patricia scooped her off her feet and carried her from the room. "Something is waiting for us, and it's very hungry! *Please!* Everyone in Widowsbury is going to die!"

Chapter Seven

The Woman with the Butterfly on Her Head

Steffen had something on his mind. He only wished he could remember what it was. It had been bothering him all week. Something to do with the park was all he could recall, and it was extremely important. The whole situation was highly upsetting because Steffen hardly ever forgot anything. He had turned nine last week. Was this a sign that he was getting old already?

All Steffen knew was that it was six o'clock in the morning, and he was wide awake just from worrying about whatever it was he'd forgotten. So, he got up, put on his coat, grabbed his knapsack, and slipped down to the park to try to retrace his steps. He brought a notepad along for his observations.

"Write everything down, my boy. It's the best way to remember things," his dad once said. He'd been talking about recipes at the time, but Steffen saw how it might apply to other occasions, too.

When he got down to the park, he reached into his knapsack and pulled out his latest invention so that he might better observe. It was a helmet—his seeing helmet, he called it—made of a mixing bowl, some miscellaneous gears and wheels, and the lenses from his opera glasses. The lenses dropped down from the brim of the helmet and fit over his own glasses, allowing him to see just about anywhere from a safe distance.

He sat down in a bed of bushes, watched, and took notes.

0615 hours: crow
0617: another crow
0620: big fat crow that looks like it ate a smaller one

Nothing sounded familiar so far. He watched and waited some more until a scratchy sort of squeal caught his attention. He held his breath. Listened.

0627: heard something

Out of the corner of his eye, he saw a flat shape waving gently forward and backward in time with the squeaks. Like a ghostly hand beckoning. Slowly his eyes rolled over to the squeaking, waving specter. He breathed a sigh of relief.

just the swing set

He adjusted the lenses on his helmet and looked farther ahead. Farther, really, than his lenses allowed, which made everything dim and blurry. He waited and watched and watched and waited, not seeing much of anything worth noting.

0629: *more crows i think*

0632: *another crow. this one is pulling a worm out of the dirt.*

"Aw, nasty!" said Steffen. He crawled out of the bushes in order to see it better, keeping cautiously low to the ground.

0635: *worm must be huge. almost looks like it has a fingerna*

Steffen stopped writing.

He sat up on the brown grass and pulled off his helmet. *I didn't see what I just saw,* he told himself. It was just a worm. And that was just a crow. Yes. It had to be.

"Caw!" squawked the crow in confirmation.

Steffen took a deep breath and put his helmet back on. Yes. That was a crow, all right, and the thing it was tugging at was definitely a worm. A very pale worm with a knuckle in its body, and a blue vein snaking through it. And a fingernail. A dirty, ragged fingernail.

"Oh gosh . . . ," Steffen whispered. He felt his stomach complain. He crawled a few paces closer and adjusted his lenses again. The worm, which was most certainly a finger, protruded from red cloth in the shape of an arm. And the arm stuck out of a large, slimy blob through which Steffen made out the unmistakable black and gold outlines of the Rudyard School logo.

"Oh. Oh gosh. Oh no . . . ," Steffen said, dread churning inside him. He stood up shakily. He had a very bad feeling that he knew just who was lying out there. This would have been an opportune time for him to turn around, run back to town, visit his father's policeman friend and tell Officer Wainscot there was a body in Widowsbury Park. But in spite of the feeling of horror welling up inside him even now, he simply couldn't walk away. His legs refused to move him any direction but forward.

He pushed the lenses up on his helmet so that he could see with his normal glasses. Then he stalked cautiously over to the slimy lump, grabbing a fallen tree branch along the way just in case the lump wasn't human at all.

As he neared it, he heard flies buzzing busily. An unmistakable stench of vomit forced him to turn his head. It smelled worse than the garbage after Goulash Day. Worse than the maggoty raccoon he found last week! Steffen steeled himself and covered his nose with his coat sleeve. Then carefully, very carefully, he poked at the slime with his branch.

It split open like a water balloon.

"Arrgh!" Steffen yelled.

Out of it spilled a mess of beetles and dead leaves and a fluid that resembled egg whites. Steffen gagged, and his eyes watered, but he peered closer still. There on the ground, covered in all that slippery muck, was Henry Fernberger II. His eyes were open. They stared up at the clouds, vacant and unblinking.

Steffen found himself unable to blink, either. He couldn't move or breathe or do anything but stare. Henry opened his mouth. Emitted a single strangled shriek. Then he shuddered and closed his eyes.

Steffen's mouth fell open. He felt a scream in his chest, but all that came out was a squawk. He dropped the tree branch and his notepad and his pen, and he turned around, running just as fast as he could. Finally, he screamed, and he screamed, and he screamed. His knapsack started to slide off his shoulders, but he let it fall. His seeing helmet toppled off his head, but he didn't stop for it. All he wanted right now was to see another person. He wouldn't even mind that person being his father, though he knew he'd be in trouble for going off the main streets. Such was his panic that he didn't even see the tall figure wearing a pink-and-white-striped apron before he ran right into it.

"*Aaaaaaaaaa!!!*" he screamed again.

Mr. Zoethout grabbed Steffen's shoulders and held the terrified boy still.

"Steffen! Steffen, it's just me! I heard noises. Are you okay? What's happened?" he asked. He knelt down to be eye level with Steffen and waited in vain for the boy to calm down.

"I saw him, Mr. Z! I saw him! I think he's dead! But he's alive! He made a sound, and his eyes were open, and there were bugs and . . . and . . . ," Steffen babbled.

"Hey, hey, slow down. It's all right," said Mr. Zoethout. Steffen looked into the candy man's cool green eyes and felt that, yes, everything was all right. Mr. Zoethout was here. Mr. Zoethout was his friend.

"Let me make sure I understand what you're saying," said Mr. Zoethout. "You found somebody? Someone you know? And he's hurt?"

Steffen nodded frantically. "He's b-back there!" he said, pointing.

Mr. Zoethout wasted no time and sprinted toward Henry. Steffen didn't want to see him again, but he wanted to be alone in the park even less, so he ran along behind.

"He's right there," said Steffen, though Mr. Zoethout was already standing over Henry. The flies scattered when Mr. Zoethout approached. Henry shuddered again, alive but unconscious.

"How in the world . . . ," Mr. Zoethout whispered. He took off his jacket, wrapped Henry up in it, and lifted the slimy bundle into his arms.

140

"We need to get him to a hospital. Can you take me there?" he asked.

Steffen nodded and led the way, grateful he hadn't had to run into town and report this on his own.

Word of Henry Fernberger's return spread through the sleepy town like wildfire. The milkman overheard Steffen's frantic cries, and he told the paperboy, who told the mailman, who told any customers who happened to be up and about at that hour of the morning. They all told their neighbors, and their neighbors told *their* neighbors, until the entire town knew by seven-fifteen a.m. that the Fernberger boy had come back, which was something of a shock to those who weren't yet aware that the son of the wealthiest family in the valley had gone missing at all.

"It's all because of the Storm!" they said, referring not to the one from the night before but the Big One, of course. It was to blame for everything bad or peculiar or just plain confusing that ever happened in Widowsbury, they felt, and this was no exception.

Unaware of all of this was Mrs. Merryweather. It was now seven-forty, and she was just getting to the point of the Breakfast Lecture.

"And, ladies, I cannot emphasize enough the value of your fortitude," she droned. "One day you shall each be of age to marry, and many of you may encounter difficulty securing a husband in these times."

Adelaide was just about to fall asleep when the *clickety-clack* of the maid running in brisk little steps down the hallway roused her. Soon the rosy-cheeked maid fluttered into the dining hall, hands flying frantically in the air.

"Headmistress Merryweather! Headmistress Merryweather!" the maid shouted in her high-pitched voice, which sounded like more of an urgent whimper.

Mrs. Merryweather dropped her hands to her sides with annoyance. "What in heaven's name is the matter, Miss Steed?" she asked.

But by the time the maid reached her destination, she was in such a state she was choking on her own words.

"Goodness gracious! Go and fetch the poor girl some water so she can tell us what's so important before she dies!" Mrs. Merryweather snapped to one of the teachers.

"It's the Fernberger boy, ma'am!" rasped the maid, once she had recovered. "He's been found, and they say he's alive!"

The dining hall immediately filled with whispers and hushed

speculations. Mrs. Merryweather gripped the corner of her podium to steady herself, one hand clutching at her heart.

"Oh, thank heaven," she whispered.

"He's at St. Bartleby's now, ma'am, and they say he's in a dreadful state!" said the maid between gulps of water.

"Thank you, Miss Steed. Thank you!" said Mrs. Merryweather, and she nodded to one of the teachers to take over the lecture as she excused herself and ran from the room.

"Wow. Did you see that? I thought Merryweather was going to faint!" Adelaide said to Maggie. Maggie only grunted as usual.

Adelaide ignored Maggie's pretense of not caring and pondered the possibilities.

"I wonder where he was," she said. "Do you think he saw Miss Delia? I just hope we can get some information from him. Er . . . and that he's okay. I imagine he has quite a story to tell."

"If he makes it at all," said Maggie.

Will Henry make it? was the question on everybody's lips that day, topped only by What happened to him, anyway? Some of the girls said that Henry had gone stark raving mad. Others said it had all been an elaborate prank.

"Phillip thinks he knows what it's all about," said Beatrice at lunch. She was remarkably calm after the previous night. Earlier she had been chattering casually about her peculiar vision as if it were little more than an interesting story she'd read.

"How is it that Phillip always knows what's going on when nobody else does?" Maggie griped.

"I don't know. He just does!" said Beatrice. "He gets bored sometimes and wanders around. He told me that Henry's asleep . . . that he went to 'the great big belly,' and that's why he's so sick right now."

"What does that even mean? What great big belly?" asked Adelaide. She was no longer certain that Phillip the Mouse was imaginary. Nor was she certain that he was real. But Beatrice had a knack for knowing things that made Adelaide wonder.

"Yeah," said Maggie. "Why does Phillip have to be so mysterious?"

"He's only a mouse, you know. He can't be expected to tell us everything!" said Beatrice.

"What about the ghost girl? Did she say anything useful or just that we're all going to die?" asked Adelaide. She was afraid that Beatrice was going to become upset again, but Beatrice only shrugged.

"Not really," she said. "She told me something wanted to eat us, and then she turned into a big scary thing, and then Nurse Özge gave me the sleepy medicine, and I had bad dreams, so I don't know which part was real anymore. But . . ."

Here she set down her fork and frowned.

"But what?" asked Adelaide.

"I'm worried," said Beatrice. "What if it wasn't a dream at all? What if there really is something out there eating people? Does that mean Miss Delia is gone forever?"

"Henry came back," said Adelaide. "If Henry came back, why couldn't Miss Delia?"

"Maybe she hasn't been fully digested," said Maggie. Adelaide hit her lightly in the shoulder.

"Nobody knows what's happening, Beatrice," said Adelaide. "The only one who might is Henry, and I'm not sure he can talk right now."

"How would we get close to him, anyway?" asked Maggie. "We can't get farther than the Wall as it is, and I don't think Steffen's going to help us anymore."

"You haven't gotten any response from Steffen at all?" Adelaide asked Beatrice, but the younger girl shook her head and sighed.

"I've sent him three notes, and Phillip swears on his grave that he delivered them all!" she insisted.

Mrs. Merryweather marched into the dining hall and took her place at the podium. There was an uncharacteristic look of cheer on her face. She sang, "Ladies!" and tapped on a water glass with a spoon.

"Ladies! Your attention please! I need everyone in the Elevens and Twelves to join me in the auditorium immediately!" she announced. "Do not go on to recess. I have something far more important planned. The rest of you will continue your day according to the usual schedule."

"Oh dear!" said Beatrice. "I hope it's not something bad!"

Adelaide promised to fill Beatrice in later. Then she and Maggie hurried to join their classmates.

In the auditorium, Mrs. Merryweather practically hummed with excitement. It would've been contagious were she not normally so stern. Now it was suspicious. Even a little disturbing.

"As I'm sure you have heard, Henry Fernberger has been found," she happily reported. "Even now, his parents are at his bedside at St. Bartleby's. However . . ."

And here her voice took on its familiar depressing tone again.

"Henry is still very gravely ill," she continued. "There is a chance that he may not improve. Therefore, I have decided that it is our task—a task the late Madame Gertrude would most assuredly have taken up herself were she still alive, God rest her—to bring cheer to Henry and his parents."

She smiled again.

"And I can think of no better cure for an ill young man than the presence of his peers!" she said in a singsong. "That is why I have chosen you girls. You're about his age, so you will better understand him. Yes, it is you, my Elevens and Twelves, who must represent Madame Gertrude's and remind both Henry and his undoubtedly strained parents that life is in store for him! Life and joy and happiness!"

She raised a fist like a general leading an army.

"Are we going to the hospital or to war?" Maggie muttered, and Adelaide had to bite her cheeks to keep from laughing.

"Do not make a fool of me in front of the Fernbergers," Mrs. Merryweather advised her audience. "Each and every one of you will be on your very best behavior or the consequences will be dire for you. I will not tolerate one single misstep! You will line up by the school doors. You will stand with your backs straight and your hands at your sides, chins up, and your shoes—which had better be polished—together. Now!"

The students stood at once and scrambled down the rows to form a line at the front. That is, except for Adelaide and Maggie, who were stopped by Mrs. Merryweather before they even made it to the front of the room.

"Not you!" was all Mrs. Merryweather said, and she pointed toward the other door. This meant they'd have to go to the playground with the other classes for recess. Or, more likely, to the Wall. Adelaide and Maggie hung their heads and did as they were told.

Until Mrs. Merryweather wasn't looking.

"We'll go up and around the side," Adelaide whispered to Maggie. They went down the hall, up the stairs to the second floor, and then out the fire escape at the side of the building, where they would be in view of neither the playground nor Mrs. Merryweather's Cheer Army.

"I knew as soon as she started talking about all this that we weren't going to be allowed to go," said Adelaide as she jumped down from the bottom rung of the fire-escape ladder.

"So, what's your plan now?" asked Maggie.

Adelaide motioned for Maggie to be quiet. She waited until she heard their classmates pass on the other side and then revealed her plan.

"We're going to follow them, but we're going to stay back. When we get inside the hospital, we can wait outside Henry's room, and I'll listen in," she said.

"What exactly do you expect to hear? He probably doesn't even know who Miss Delia is."

"Why are you always so negative? At least there's a chance!" Adelaide snapped. "Look, I think Henry knows something. Even if he hasn't seen Miss Delia, I'd be pretty surprised if his disappearance and Miss Delia's aren't related."

"If you say so," Maggie muttered doubtfully, but she followed along just the same.

St. Bartleby's Hospital was a windowless white box with a minty green interior that reminded Adelaide of toothpaste. The place was often referred to as "the graveyard," and though neither Adelaide nor Maggie had been there before, they already had a keen sense of why. It was dead quiet in there. The nurses kept themselves completely covered in white surgical masks and white caps over white hairnets, and their white dresses were so long that their feet didn't show as they whooshed, ghostlike, from one room to another. Each room had a number on its door, but the numbers were in no logical order. People said it was because the numbers were actually a count of patients who had died in there. People said a lot of things in Widowsbury. Unfortunately, many of those things were true.

Adelaide and Maggie ducked into a side corridor as they waited for their classmates to file into Henry's room. Adelaide was just pressing her ear to a wall when the hair on her neck rose, and she promptly felt Maggie elbow her in the back. She looked up and nearly screamed.

"Aren't you girls from the school?" said a nurse, muffled by her mask.

"No," said Maggie.

"Yes! We are, ma'am. I think we're lost. Can you tell us where our class has gone?" Adelaide blurted.

The nurse wordlessly pointed to the open door of Room 12 (which was next door to Rooms 72 and 804). Adelaide thanked the nurse before grabbing Maggie's arm and dragging her along.

They slipped into the room at the back of the crowd of some twenty-four students, all packed so tightly that some of the girls had to sit on Henry's bed. The boy himself lay unconscious and pale. Every now and then, he twitched, but that was the only sign of life.

It was then that the Fernbergers returned with the decrepit old Dr. Warden, long gray coat buttoned up to his chin and dark glasses completely concealing his sensitive eyes. Also accompanying them was, of all people, Mr. Zoethout. Mr. Zoethout winked at Adelaide and Maggie and placed a finger over his lips as if to say he knew they weren't supposed to be there, but their secret was safe with him.

"What are all these *urchins* doing in our son's room?" asked the rotund Mr. Fernberger, fumbling with his necktie. His hawkish wife clutched protectively at her pearls.

Mrs. Merryweather pushed through the throng of school-children and proudly introduced herself.

"I am the headmistress of Madame Gertrude's School for Girls," she said with an exaggerated curtsy. "We are an institution that has benefited greatly from your generosity, Mr. and Mrs. Fernberger. When we heard the news of poor Henry, we were simply beside

ourselves with worry! Therefore, we have come to help speed his recovery with the timeless medicine of good cheer!"

The Fernbergers blinked. Mr. Zoethout had to stifle his laughter. The cranky old Dr. Warden turned scarlet with anger.

"You fool!" he shouted in a surprisingly powerful voice for such a frail-looking person. Mrs. Merryweather's mouth fell open.

"Who told you to bring all these children in here?!" the doctor shouted.

"I th-thought young Henry could use a f-few visitors," Mrs. Merryweather stammered.

Dr. Warden was not appeased.

"Get them out of here!" he shouted.

Mrs. Merryweather was aghast. "Dr. Warden, I really must protest! These girls are his peers! How else do you expect him to recover?"

Dr. Warden coughed raucously and spat into a handkerchief. "I don't care who they are!" he shouted. "You're endangering the boy's health. You're endangering the health of your girls! You're endangering my health by testing my patience! I want everybody out of here except for the parents!"

Mrs. Merryweather stumbled over her apologies and began herding her students from the room.

Dr. Warden turned to Mr. Zoethout. "You too, candy man!" he snarled. "You did your good deed for the day. Now get out!"

Mr. Zoethout tipped his hat to the students and then turned to leave, but Mrs. Fernberger caught his arm.

"I just wanted to tell you how much Charles and I appreciate your bringing Henry in, Mr. Zoethout," she said with a slight blush. "I—we would be delighted to have you up at the house anytime."

Mr. Fernberger nodded in agreement and then jealously took his wife's arm.

"Certainly!" said Mr. Zoethout. "Wow. I'd be delighted to visit, ma'am!"

"And you must bring more of your specialties!" added Mr. Fernberger, patting his bulging stomach and grinning.

Mr. Zoethout laughed. "You bet, sir!" he said. Then he bid his goodbyes and departed.

"Come along, girls," Mrs. Merryweather said softly. With her pride shattered before the Fernbergers, she seemed almost half her size. It even looked for a moment as if she was going to cry.

Suddenly Henry awoke and let out a violent scream. Everyone stopped.

"They're all dead! Dead! The horse monsters! No! Leave me alone! Leave me alone! I can't keep my eyes open! The carousel! Everything's going so fast!" he screamed, his face contorted in agony.

Dr. Warden rushed to his bedside and felt the boy's forehead.

"The fever's gone up," he said. "Didn't I tell you all to *get out?*"

Mrs. Merryweather began to push her students out the door. Henry opened his eyes and grabbed on to Dr. Warden's arm. "It was her!" he said, his eyes wide and his hair plastered to his forehead with sweat. "She helped me! The woman with the butterfly on her head! Then the horse monsters got her! They got her!"

He threw himself back on the bed and let out an unholy wail.

"The butterfly pin!" Adelaide whispered.

Mrs. Fernberger forced her way through the mass of people leaving the room and took her son's hand, but he pulled away, still shrieking. Adelaide no longer cared if she was caught by Mrs. Merryweather or Dr. Warden. She pushed back into the room.

"What woman? What did she look like? Was she Miss Delia? Did you see Miss Delia where you were? Is she still alive?" she asked frantically. Mrs. Merryweather abruptly pulled her back.

"Leave him alone, Miss Foss!" she snapped. "Did you not hear what Dr. Warden said? You'll make Henry sick! You're not even supposed to be here as it is!"

She shoved Adelaide out the door, where Maggie was waiting.

"I have to get back in there!" said Adelaide, but Maggie stopped her.

"It won't help," she said. "He's out of his head anyway! Let's go."

Adelaide, crestfallen, relented and the two of them joined their classmates in the journey back to their school. Even as they walked outside, they could hear Henry's screams.

Mrs. Merryweather said nothing as they walked. She didn't even bother to threaten Adelaide and Maggie for disobeying her. She seemed shrunken. Weary. She had been mortified in front of the Fernbergers and, worse, in front of her students, and it had humbled her. Or, at least, momentarily stunned her.

As they neared the school, they were met by a junior teacher who went pale the moment she saw them.

"Miss Clara, I want you to take them to recess. I have . . . matters to attend to," Mrs. Merryweather said almost inaudibly.

"But recess is already over, Mrs. Merryweather. The girls are lining up to go back indoors," said Miss Clara, her small eyes looking large and beady through her thick glasses.

"Extend it!" Mrs. Merryweather snarled. "Let it go on until the Evening Hobby. That is all I have to say on the matter!"

She threw her hand up dismissively and stormed into the school, leaving the bewildered Miss Clara with the students.

"Come along, ladies," said Miss Clara, wringing her hands. "That's . . . quite a reward! You all must have made her very proud!"

The girls obediently followed the young teacher back to the doors of Madame Gertrude's. Adelaide looked over at Maggie and drew her hand across her forehead.

"Whew!" she whispered. "I thought for sure we'd end up in you-know-where for that."

"Don't count your chickens. We're not in the clear yet," said Maggie.

The two girls in front of them turned around and stared Adelaide up and down reproachfully.

"Can I help you?" said Maggie, and the girls quickly faced ahead again.

"Did you hear what Henry said?" Adelaide whispered. "He described Miss Delia. I know that was her. She's alive somewhere!"

"Yeah, and then he said some horse monsters got her," said Maggie. "It doesn't make any sense, Adelaide. All we heard in there was a sick kid's feverish babbling."

Adelaide was about to protest when she froze.

"Shh!" she said. Maggie stopped. Something was moving in the bushes behind them.

"Hey! Adelaide! Maggie! It's me!" said that something, which turned out to be Steffen in homemade camouflage.

Adelaide and Maggie walked slower and slower, until they were certain their classmates weren't aware they were missing, then tiptoed back to the shrubbery.

"I was starting to think you weren't going to talk to us anymore!" Adelaide whispered.

"I got over it," answered Steffen. "But that's not what I wanted to tell you. I wanted to tell you that I remembered! Miss Delia. She went to the park! And so did Henry! And there's more, but I have to show you. Are you coming?"

Adelaide looked at Maggie, who shrugged. Whatever they did was fine by her as long as somebody hurried up and made a decision.

"That's great news, but I'm not sure if we can, Steffen. It's really a wonder we're not in trouble as it is!" said Adelaide.

"Trust me! You need to see this," said Steffen. "It's the thing that got them. I think I found it!"

- CHAPTER EIGHT -
Something Is Very Displeased

S teffen rummaged through his knapsack and retrieved two china soup bowls with leather belts, copper wires, and bits of fishing tackle attached.

"Put these on!" he told them.

"What are they?" asked Maggie with a look of disgust.

"Invisibility helmets! They're my latest invention. I haven't been able to test them properly yet, but it's worth a try," Steffen answered.

The girls strapped on their helmets, which, not surprisingly, did not work at all.

"Oh well," said Steffen. "At least I know. It's hard to test these things yourself when people pretend they can't see you as it is. Anyway, follow me, and try not to be obvious."

They followed Steffen to Widowsbury Park, ignoring the questioning looks of townsfolk who doubtlessly wondered what three children—two of whom were newcomers by Widowsburian standards—could be up to, out of school in the middle of the day.

When they reached their destination, Steffen motioned for them to be quiet.

"It's in the woods," he said.

"We're not actually going in there, are we?" asked Adelaide.

"We'll stop just at the border, I promise, but trust me! You've gotta see this," said Steffen.

Maggie tensed and rolled up her sleeves. Just in case it came to that.

It was a very odd thing, how starkly the atmosphere changed once one crossed the border between the park and the woods. It was as if someone had drawn a line in the perpetually brown lawn of the park and said, *All right. This is ours. The rest is for evil.* It wasn't merely the landscape that changed. The sky was actually darker in the woods. The park sounded miles away even if one stood exactly at the edge. Here the trees reached their naked limbs up and scratched at the dark sky, distortions in the bark making faces paralyzed in anguish. Mist crept low to the ground, curling around each whispering tree as if searching for something it had lost.

"What did you want us to see, Steffen? I don't like it here," said Adelaide. Her arms had turned to goose bumps, and a feeling in her gut told her danger was very near. The sooner they got this over with, the better.

"Here," said Steffen, pointing to a place on the ground where the dead grass had been flattened. It was still a little slimy. "This is where I found Henry."

"*You* found Henry?" said Maggie.

"I didn't mean to," Steffen said guiltily. He was used to feeling guilty for something or other.

Adelaide swallowed. "What happened?" she asked.

"He screamed. It was awful!" Steffen recounted. "Then Mr. Zoethout came over, and we took Henry to the hospital. I guess I dropped a bunch of my things in all the excitement, so I had to come back later and get them."

He pointed ahead, into the black trees of the woods. "That's when I noticed this trail."

They looked. Sure enough, there was a narrow but very clear path cut into the brush.

"And?" said Maggie.

"*And* it wasn't there a few days ago!" said Steffen. "You might not understand it, but in Widowsbury, everything new is announced and then announced again in case anybody missed it the first time. Something hidden like this could be something bad. But that's not all."

Steffen pulled his seeing helmet from his bag and handed it to Adelaide.

"Put that on," he said. "No, this one works. I promise."

Adelaide did as he directed, then adjusted the strap beneath her chin and turned the little rings around the lenses that descended in front of her face.

"Look down the path. What do you see?" asked Steffen.

Adelaide looked. At first she saw nothing, but then, almost blending into the sky, was a blurry white square with red blotches on it. She adjusted the lenses again.

"It's some sort of sign," she said.

"Read it," said Steffen. Adelaide squinted to make out the shapes of the letters. It said:

GRAND OPENING THIS FRIDAY AT 3 O'CLOCK! SEE THE MYSTERIES OF THE WORLD! EXPERIENCE THE THRILL OF THE SCIENCES! RIDE THE CAROUSEL! FREE FOR ALL AGES!

"A carousel!" she exclaimed.

"Exactly," said Steffen, "and Widowsbury's never *had* a carousel."

Below the words was a bright red arrow pointing down. Adelaide followed the arrow until she made out a brightly polished golden dome. In the panels of the dome were ovals, each of which contained a painting of a different person, none of whom looked particularly happy to be there.

She pulled off the seeing helmet and tossed it to Maggie.

"Do you see it?" she said.

"It's like you said," Maggie agreed after looking. She took a few steps forward to see it better.

"No! Wait! It's not safe!" said Steffen. "It's involved in Henry's disappearance somehow. It has to be!"

"A little kid's ride?" Maggie scoffed. She returned Steffen's helmet.

"Didn't you pay any attention to Henry's shouting?" asked Adelaide. "He specifically said there was a carousel!"

Maggie looked into the woods and tilted her head.

"All right. I get that it might be happening near the carousel, but I don't get how it *is* the carousel unless there's some kind of trapdoor or something," she said.

"That's the thing," said Steffen. "I don't think it's just a carousel. Henry looked like he'd been somewhere terrible. He was covered in slimy stuff when I found him, and he smelled bad. Like he'd been thrown up."

Adelaide remembered what Beatrice had told them about Phillip. "The great big belly . . . ," she recalled.

"Er, yes," said Steffen, not quite understanding. "What I'm trying to say is, I think the carousel is hiding something worse. What else would it be doing here?"

Maggie wasn't so certain. "Wouldn't somebody have noticed the carousel by now?" she said. "With all the search parties going on lately, surely someone would have crossed its path."

"That's what I can't figure out," said Steffen.

Adelaide ducked. "Someone's coming!"

Steffen and Maggie darted into the bushes beside her.

"I don't hear anythi—" Steffen started to say.

"Hush," Maggie interrupted. "She does."

Adelaide closed her eyes and made a face like she was concentrating very hard.

"It's a little kid, I think," she whispered, "but she's alone. She's very small. Too small to be out here by herself."

Adelaide's observation proved true as a little girl, no older than four, ran down the path past their hiding place. Her blond pigtails bounced happily with each step as she ambled along, slurping a rainbow-colored lollipop and humming a tune only she could know.

"Why aren't there any grown-ups with her? My dad didn't let me go anywhere by myself until I was six!" Steffen whispered.

The child looked up, laughed, and took off at a clumsy sprint down the pathway.

"Looks like she found the carousel, all right," said Maggie.

"We have to stop her!" Adelaide cried. She sprang out of the bushes, ignoring the scratchy thorns, and chased after the child at lightning speed, swooping her up off the path so fast the little girl was not aware her feet were in the air.

Steffen's mouth fell open. "Does she practice a lot or something?" he asked.

Maggie climbed out from the shrubbery and plucked a few twigs out of her hair.

"Nah. She just does things like that," she answered.

"Where's your mommy?" Adelaide was asking the little girl when the others caught up. But the girl was evidently not interested in conversation.

"See the horses!" she squealed, pointing with a chubby pink finger.

"No, you don't want to see the horses. Those are bad horses. People have gotten hurt on those," said Adelaide. The child wriggled free of Adelaide's arms and jumped to the ground.

"See the horses!" she screeched, at such a high pitch it made Adelaide double over and cover her ears in pain.

With the barrier of Adelaide out of the way, the child raced toward the carousel, giggling and squealing, with Maggie and Steffen chasing hopelessly after.

"I can't catch up to her! She's too fast!" Steffen shouted. Maggie stumbled on a rock in the path and clattered awkwardly to the ground.

"Wait!" she called out as she scrambled to her feet.

The child was toddling up to the carousel. Steffen stopped short and took a step backward.

The little girl had climbed onto one of the horses and was patting it gently on the head.

Maggie skidded into place beside Steffen. "Are we too late?" she said.

The child let out an ear-splitting peal of laughter and clung to the horse's neck as if she were flying through the air, even though the carousel wasn't moving at all.

"False alarm. It looks like nothing's going to happen," said Steffen.

"Hold on, I'm coming!" Adelaide called. She steadied herself, shook the ringing out of her ears, and joined the others. They watched the little girl for a while, but apart from an overactive imagination, she seemed to be fine.

And then the girl yawned, rested her head on the horse's neck, and with no particular effect, simply ceased to be.

"Whoa! What just happened?" said Adelaide.

"She just . . . ! But wh-where . . . what j-j-just . . . !" Steffen stammered.

"I didn't see any trapdoors," Maggie muttered.

"I didn't see any *anything*!" said Steffen.

Adelaide cautiously walked all around the carousel.

"But it didn't move!" she insisted. "There wasn't anybody else around it! She just went *poof!* Right in front of us!"

"I don't think we should get any closer," Steffen warned.

Adelaide looked to the others. There was fear in her eyes. Plain as a cloudless day in the days when Widowsbury still had them.

"This is bad," she said. "This is beyond us, and it's definitely bigger than Miss Delia. We have to get help!"

"Yeah, but who's going to listen to us?" said Maggie. "Who's going to believe we saw some kid just vanish into thin air, huh?"

"Everyone, actually," Steffen answered. "Then they'll all hide in their cellars and not come out until it goes away by itself."

Adelaide's head was starting to hurt. It was all too much to comprehend. People gone missing. People coming back delirious. A carousel that made little girls disappear.

"It's not as if we can handle this ourselves. We have to tell someone!" Adelaide said. "Aren't there any policemen around? Don't they have some kind of training for this sort of thing? They'd have to in this town!"

"Officer Wainscot is a friend of my dad's," offered Steffen. "He's always been nice. If anyone will help us, it's him. He's usually walking around in front of the bank on Greengage Avenue."

Adelaide, Maggie, and Steffen ran from the woods, down Damson Street, taking a turn at Greengage, where they found Officer Wainscot walking up and down the sidewalk, looking for people who might be walking too fast or too slow or with any other oddness in their step.

"Steffen Weller!" he greeted jovially. His breath smelled of lemon drops. "And you've got some friends with you, I see. Tell me. How's your old dad?"

"He's fine, Officer Wainscot, but—" Steffen started.

"You know, the missus has been bothering me to ask him about his flapjacks recipe. Won't let me get a wink of sleep until I promise to ask, and I always forget—"

"Officer Wainscot, please! We need help!" Adelaide interrupted.

"All right. All right," said Officer Wainscot. "What seems to be the trouble? One of you skin your knee?"

"It's the woods, sir," said Steffen. "We found a carousel out there. Don't know who put it there. But it's bad, sir. We saw a little girl get on it and she just . . . she just . . ."

"She disappeared!" Adelaide finished. "Right in front of us!"

Suddenly Officer Wainscot looked very serious, and he twisted his silver beard in a very serious way. "Disappeared, you say? On a carousel? Didn't know we had a carousel in Widowsbury," he said.

"We don't!" said Steffen. "I mean, the town didn't put it there. I think it's where Henry Fernberger might have gone. Maybe Cornelius Patterson and the handyman from the girls' school, too!"

"And our librarian! Don't forget about Miss Delia!" Adelaide reminded him.

Officer Wainscot narrowed his eyes, thinking. He twisted his beard in the other direction.

"Show me where you saw it," he instructed, and he pulled a slip of paper and a pencil from under his cap.

Finally! thought Adelaide.

"What did she look like, this little girl you saw?" asked Officer

165

Wainscot as they walked. They told him, and he jotted down the details.

"Was anyone with her?" he asked next.

Then, "How old would you say she was? Not twelve, I hope. That's a bad-luck age."

And, "About this carousel, was anyone else on it?"

Now they stood at the edge of Henbane Wood. Even Officer Wainscot hesitated before entering.

"Come on. It's this way," said Steffen.

Officer Wainscot popped another lemon drop into his mouth and went back to his questions. "You're sure you didn't meet anyone unusual along the way?" he asked, the lemon drop clacking against his teeth.

And, "You didn't see any sort of opening or door on it?"

Then, "What's your favorite color?"

They stopped.

"My favorite what?" asked Steffen.

"Mine is blue, so you can't have that one," said the officer with a giggle. "What's your favorite number?"

"But, Officer Wainscot, this is important!" said Adelaide.

"Say twelve! Go on, say it!" the officer chanted, and he started to prance around them in circles.

Maggie and Adelaide turned to Steffen, who simply stared.

"Officer Wainscot, people are missing. They need your help!" he said.

Officer Wainscot stomped his foot. "I don't want to look for the girl anymore," he said, pouting.

"But you're a policeman!" said Maggie.

"You know what I think? I think *you* lost her," said the officer.

"What?!" Adelaide exclaimed.

"She wasn't ours to begin with," said Maggie.

Steffen was too shocked to say anything.

"Don't you at least want to investigate? Report it? Something?" asked Adelaide.

The policeman stuck out his tongue. "No!" he said. "You can't make me!"

The children looked at each other, thoroughly and completely dumbfounded.

"What's wrong with you? You're an officer of the law!" said Adelaide. She'd never spoken to a policeman that way, but Officer Wainscot was acting nothing like a policeman and everything like, well, a little kid. It wasn't just offensive. It was downright weird.

"Fine," Officer Wainscot huffed. "Here's your report!" and he showed them his paper. All it had on it was a crudely drawn stick figure farting.

"Is everyone going completely insane?" asked Adelaide.

Officer Wainscot yawned. "You're boring," he said, and he pranced off through the trees without them.

Maggie grabbed her companions by their arms and pulled them away from the woods.

"Something tells me we should get out of here," she said.

Steffen was in utter shock. "I'm scared. Really scared!" he said. "I've never seen him act like that. I've known him my whole life!"

Maggie glanced back, worried. "He can't help us, and if *he* can't help us, I'm not sure who will," she said.

"It seemed to get worse the closer we got to the woods," said Adelaide. "Like there's something in the air. Except it didn't affect *us*. We have to warn people somehow. It's going to keep doing what it does until someone stops it, and until someone stops it, we have to make people stay away!"

"Yes, but again, who's going to listen to us? Even if they believe we found a people-stealing carousel, they're only going to assume we're the problem. No one's ever going to pay us any attention," said Maggie.

Steffen thought for a second. "I know what we can do!" he said. He opened his knapsack and pulled out a crumpled flyer he'd once saved for scratch paper. The front side said PANIC WILL COST YOU! PLAY A PRANK AND PAY THE PRICE! $50 FINE! with the printed seal and a photograph of Mayor Templeton below it.

"Watch this," he said. He pulled a black fountain pen from his bag. Then he folded the flyer so that the blank side covered the front just enough to leave the mayor's seal and picture visible. He wrote as neatly as he could manage:

AVOID THE WOODS AT ALL COSTS. STAY AWAY
FROM THE CAROUSEL! STAY CLOSE TO LIFE!

"Stay close to life?" said Maggie.

"What? It's the best I could do on short notice," Steffen sniffed.

"It's fine," said Adelaide. "Even if they don't believe it's from the mayor, they'll start asking questions, and either way, someone will find out what's going on over here. Steffen? Maggie and I have to get back to the school before they start to miss us. If it's not too late. Can you make more of these signs?"

Steffen nodded proudly. "There will be at least fifty of these things nailed all over town by nightfall, I guarantee it," he boasted.

"Good. And good luck," said Adelaide. Then she and Maggie ran as fast as they could back to Madame Gertrude's. Steffen hurried into town, pulling flyers off trees and walls and wherever he could find them. The flyers were meant to be distributed, he told himself, and his warnings were much more serious than the usual paranoid doom and gloom. That made it all right, didn't it?

169

In Henbane Wood, a tall and strangely shadowy man emerged from the trees. He inhaled deeply and exhaled slowly, stretching his long fingers at his sides, each knuckle cracking like kindling in his gloves.

"Determined little saplings, aren't they?" he said. "And so *difficult*. No matter. We'll just have to take extra precautions. Won't we, Officer Wainscot?"

Beside him, Officer Wainscot cowered, tears streaming down his grizzled face.

"I don't want to see the monsters anymore! Please, mister, get them out of my head! I want to see my puppy again!" he blubbered. The shadow man took the policeman's cap and twirled it on his finger. Then he flipped it around backward and placed it on the officer's head with a pat.

"I'll let you play again soon," he said, "but only if you're a good boy and finish your chores."

Officer Wainscot nodded vigorously, wiping his nose on his uniform sleeve.

"Now," said the shadow man, checking his watch, "bring me Mayor Templeton."

The afternoon turned to dusk and dusk to starless nightfall. Storm clouds formed ripples across the black sky like the curtains of a hearse. Flyers with Steffen's warnings fluttered as they were torn from their posts by nature and thrown to the wild. Even the tree branches trembled. Then there was a long, drawn-out whisper as the wind hushed the streetlamps, lulling their little orange lights to sleep. All was in darkness. Only the owls had the courage to speak, their hooting answered by the faraway wail of a phantom train.

Midnight.

Adelaide had long been asleep, her slumber riddled with nightmares about carousels and lost children. In her dream, she saw the little girl again. Her perfect golden pigtails bounced as she jumped onto the carousel in slow motion. Adelaide tried to catch her, but her legs just wouldn't move. The little girl stopped and turned, and Adelaide saw that her eyes were lemon yellow, and her fingernails had gotten long and sharp. She lifted a finger to one of the carousel poles and scratched, scratched, scratched.

That was when Adelaide woke up. But still she heard the scratching sound. The sound came from somewhere outside, though just where outside was difficult to discern over the tap dance of rain.

She slipped out of bed and padded over to the window. Carefully and quietly she drew back one of the heavy brown velvet drapes and peered out. It was raining buckets out there. Thunder threatened, chasing after lightning that turned the clouds green with every strike. *Wait a minute*, thought Adelaide. *What's wrong with the lightning?*

Something about it was abnormal, but her groggy head couldn't quite figure it out just yet. She let the drapes fall closed again and padded across the room to Maggie's bedside.

"I'm already awake. You don't have to shake me," Maggie said softly. She was staring up at the ceiling.

"You can't sleep, either?" asked Adelaide.

"Obviously not," said Maggie, but the expression on her face was one of worry and not her usual sarcasm.

"Come and look out the window. There's something odd about the storm, but I can't put my finger on it," Adelaide whispered.

Maggie followed her to the window and peeked through the curtains just as another finger of lightning speared the clouds. Then it dawned on Adelaide just why it was wrong.

"Did you see that?" she said.

Maggie watched it. "It's backward or something," she said.

"It's striking from the ground up. From the same spot," said Adelaide, pointing. "Look, there it goes again!"

Their faces were illuminated in green as they watched.

"That's the park. That's where the carousel is," said Adelaide.

It came at faster intervals now, scratching at the clouds with electric fingers. There was a squeaking sound like an army of rats coming up the road. In the sky, they saw a moving mass of black things aglow in the flashes.

"Bats!" said Adelaide just as a swarm of the creatures flapped frantically past the window as though fleeing something far more rabid than themselves.

"Bats flying through the streets, backward lightning, bad dreams. What's next?" she wondered aloud.

Maggie pointed to the opposite end of the street. "Down there," she said. At least a dozen scattered people, mostly adults but a couple of small children, too, wandered through the mud and rain in nothing but their pajamas.

"What are they doing?" asked Adelaide. "They don't even have shoes on, most of them!"

"I think we can guess where they're headed," said Maggie.

The people were all moving in the same direction, and all of them as slow as the walking dead. Adelaide hurriedly unlatched the window and then opened it.

"Hey!" she called out into the storm, but it was no use. "I don't think they can hear us out there," she said.

She gently latched the window and wiped the rainwater from her face. In the back of the dormitory, one of her dorm mates groaned and then fell asleep again.

"I'm not sure they even know they're doing it. Look at the way they're moving," said Maggie. "Like they're sleepwalking or somebody's got them all on strings."

"We should stop them," said Adelaide.

"We can't. We already know that," said Maggie.

"Can't we tell somebody, at least?"

"Like Officer Wainscot? Right."

Adelaide felt very small and helpless now, caught in the center of something supremely awful that she couldn't stop. And she had only wanted to find the nice librarian lady to get her job back. It seemed so naive now.

"Get back!" whispered Maggie. She ducked behind the curtain and pointed to the opposite end of the street, where something dark was moving.

At first, it seemed to be a shadow of a very tall man. It stretched and writhed, this shadow, and it was as tall as a house. But it soon became apparent that it wasn't a shadow of a man. It *was* a man. He was a giant but razor thin. He had the unnatural, elongated look of a person standing on stilts, except the stilts were his legs. His arms were stretched as he dragged his claws along the windows and doors of buildings he passed. When he grinned, his teeth glittered in the moonlight. Except it wasn't the moonlight, it was the light of his eyes. Two yellow rings beaming in the darkness.

It was as if he knew they were watching him.

He jerked his head and looked up at them, then began humming a strange tune.

"Shut the curtains! Shut the curtains!" Maggie whispered, but Adelaide couldn't move.

The man marched rubber-legged toward them, his arms and legs growing and shrinking and growing and shrinking. The faster he moved, the faster he hummed.

"He's coming! Get down!" Maggie hissed. Adelaide snapped out of it and closed the curtains just before the strange man reached their sixth-floor window.

"Who is he? *What* is he?" Adelaide asked.

"Pretty sure I don't want to find out," said Maggie.

They waited anxiously, afraid to sit so close to the window but afraid to go anywhere else.

The scratching started again.

Scratch.

It was right outside their building.

Scritch.

Now it was on their window.

Scratch tap. Scratch tap.

Tap.

Tap.

"Maggie?" Adelaide whispered. Maggie reached over and squeezed her hand. They sat in the darkness, trying not to breathe too loudly until the noises stopped.

"Is he gone?" asked Maggie.

Adelaide slowly stood and peeled back one curtain.

She gasped and fell backward.

The strange man's face was pressed up against the glass, and he grinned at them toothily. He was so terribly pale, and his lips were so red they looked painted. At the base of the window, a handful of cockroaches fled their hiding places in the bricks and scurried across the dormitory floor. The man held up his claw-hands and opened them with eerie grace. Floating between them was a monarch butterfly haloed by the yellow light of his eyes.

"Miss Delia . . . ," Adelaide said. "He knows where she is! We've got to open the window!"

She unlatched the window again and had started to open it when Maggie slapped her hands away, locked the window, and pulled the drapes shut.

"Are you crazy?" Adelaide hissed.

"It's a trap!" whispered Maggie. "That man knows of Miss Delia because he's the one who took her! And you almost let him get us, too!"

They heard a sound like a bird beating its wings against the window, and then it was quiet. Adelaide shuddered and sank down to the floor again.

"I did, didn't I?" she said with a lost look. "I don't know what came over me. I don't know what's going on anymore. Things like this don't happen anywhere else I've been. I think I'm scared. I thought I was braver than that."

"It doesn't matter if you're brave or not. Just don't go near the window. Okay?" said Maggie. Adelaide nodded.

They sat on the cold stone floor and waited without another sound. Eventually the drapes stopped glowing with the distant bursts of lightning. The thunder stopped rumbling, and the rain ebbed into a few scattered drops.

"Get up, Foss and Borland! What are you doing on the floor? You'll ruin your posture that way!" barked the all-too familiar voice of Miss Patricia.

It was six-thirty in the morning. They hadn't even realized they'd fallen asleep. Adelaide and Maggie scrambled to their feet and hoped no one else noticed. Miss Patricia harrumphed and went to attend to other matters.

Adelaide pulled back the drapes.

"Maggie!" she cried out. "You'd better see this!"

There, pasted to the center of the window, was a flyer advertising a fair for the grand opening of a carousel. At the bottom, beside an official seal, it said MAYOR TEMPLETON SAYS: APPROVED! SAFE! A-OK!

It was stuck in the middle of a butterfly that had been drawn with mud.

"It's a message," said Adelaide.

"It's a threat," said Maggie.

Someone poked Adelaide in the elbow. Expecting it to be one of her dorm mates picking on her as usual, Adelaide said, "Hey!" and spun around. But it was only Beatrice.

She looked paler than usual, and she was shaking.

"Are you all right?" asked Adelaide.

Beatrice tried very, very hard not to cry, but her eyes were betraying her. "Margret visited me again last night, and this time I know it wasn't a dream," she said, her voice barely above a whisper. "She told me that something is very displeased with us."

Adelaide gulped. She had a sinking feeling inside.

"Adelaide?" Beatrice asked. "What did you do?"

- CHAPTER NINE -
A Friend

Beatrice saw the flyer stuck to the window. She saw the butterfly. She was just about to ask more questions when she saw a familiar blond head entering the school below.

"Oh, look," said Beatrice, pointing. "It's Steffen!"

She tapped on the glass and waved to him. It took some time before he noticed that the sound was coming from above. He looked up, put a finger over his lips. Then he disappeared inside the school.

"What's he being all secretive for? He comes in and out all the time," said Adelaide.

Within minutes, the alarm bells sounded.

"Probably that," said Maggie.

The Elevens and Twelves scattered throughout the dorm, hurriedly pulling on shoes and dresses and coats in a panic.

"Hurry up! Get your shoes on and line up in an orderly fashion!" Miss Patricia ordered.

"What's happened?" asked one of the other girls.

"Search me," Miss Patricia groused. "Something about the

kitchen going mad. Pull yourselves together and go down to the auditorium. Go on! Get going!"

She either did not notice or didn't care that Beatrice was among the older girls. The students clamored and whispered and shouted until they somehow managed to form an orderly line, whereupon they filed out to the hallway and down the stairs. Adelaide, Beatrice, and Maggie, as usual, were the last to leave.

"Psst!" came a whisper from behind them just as they made it down the first flight.

Naturally, it was Steffen. He put his finger to his lips again and led them outside through the side door and down the fire escape.

"What's going on?" asked Beatrice when they made it to the ground.

"I created a diversion!" said Steffen, remembering something they always said in the adventure stories. Then he added mysteriously, "And that's all you need to know. Now come with me."

"Are we going to get in trouble?" asked Beatrice.

Maggie snorted.

"Probably, but not in the way you're thinking," said Adelaide.

The four ran down the street, past the shops and houses, and down toward Widowsbury Park.

"No!" Adelaide cried. Nailed to every lamppost, building, fence, and even on the doorways of homes were flyers. They were identical to the one stuck on the dorm window only that morning. The entire town had been invited.

Steffen nodded knowingly. "The tall man?"

"You saw him, too!" Adelaide said excitedly. "We saw a bunch of people walking off toward the park last night. Like they were under some sort of spell. And then that man came, and he tried to make us go outside with the others!"

"She just about let him in, too," said Maggie.

"He tricked me. That's not fair," said Adelaide.

"He tried to make me come outside as well, but I piled all my books up in front of the window," said Steffen, "and there's something else."

He stopped and pulled from his bag a vial of rainwater and unstopped it.

"Smell it," he said.

Adelaide could already smell it without having to go near it. She scrunched up her nose. "Smells like . . . burnt sugar."

"It's sticky like sugar, too, but I wouldn't dare taste it," said Steffen.

He held it out to Maggie and Beatrice, who both declined to sniff it.

"Tell him about your visitor, Beatrice," said Adelaide.

Beatrice squirmed. She didn't like to talk about her visitors, but she could see that it was important.

"There's a ghost girl who keeps coming to me," she said. "She gives me messages, and I think they're warnings. Her name is Margret. She says something is hungry. I think people are . . ."

She grimaced and whispered something in Adelaide's ear.

"She thinks people are being eaten, but she doesn't like to say so," Adelaide said.

Steffen shook his head. "This whole nightmare just gets weirder and weirder the deeper we go," he said.

Beatrice frowned. "I still don't know what any of you are talking about. You promised you'd tell me about it yesterday, but you didn't!"

"It's a long story, Beatrice," said Maggie.

"To make it short, we think we got a little too close to the truth," said Adelaide. "That thing that's eating people? We think it's hiding in the woods. Inside a carousel."

Beatrice bit her fingernails. "We're going back there, aren't we?"

The girls looked at Steffen.

"I have a plan" was all he said.

They walked on in silence until they reached the woods and the hulking shape of the carousel. It seemed bigger than when they last saw it.

Beatrice stared at it long and hard.

"It's her," she said softly. She pointed to one of the portraits of sad people on the carousel's canopy. "The Other Ghost. Margret. She looks like the one in the center."

The largest portrait was of a girl who appeared to be fourteen or fifteen years old, with perfect spirals of glossy brown hair. She wore a pink dress, and she looked as serious as the grave.

Steffen stepped in front of them, blocking Beatrice's view of the girl.

"Listen," he said, pleased at how like his father he sounded. "We don't have time for distractions right now. I brought you all out here because I have a plan. I don't know how to stop whatever's happening, but I think we can get those answers. Maybe from the carousel itself."

He pulled a long, thick rope from his knapsack.

"What's that for?" asked Adelaide.

"The carousel makes people disappear, right?" said Steffen. They agreed.

"And if Henry came back . . . ," he went on.

"Then it must be taking them somewhere!" Adelaide finished.

"Right," said Steffen. "We need to go there, too, if we want to help anyone it's taken, but we can't just jump on there and go for a ride. We have to get back somehow. So, we tie this around one of us. That person gets on the carousel, and the others stay behind."

"Then what?" asked Maggie.

"That lucky person lets the carousel take 'em," said Steffen, as simply as if he were explaining how a toaster works. "Then we wait, holding on to the rope. If they don't come back pretty quick, we pull them back. Got it?"

"Yeah . . . ," said Adelaide thoughtfully. "Yeah, that might work!"

"Just what do you think you children are doing?" said a man's voice from behind them. They screamed in surprise, but it was only Mr. Zoethout, his arms folded across his chest. He looked very stern and disapproving and not at all like his usual friendly self.

"It's okay!" said Steffen. "It's just Mr. Z! We can trust him."

"I haven't made up my mind about that just yet," said Adelaide. She had a very bad feeling at the moment that she couldn't explain. Perhaps she was simply startled, she considered. But then how had she not heard him approach in those woods, with all the dry leaves and brush everywhere?

Mr. Zoethout dropped his arms from his chest, but he remained unsmiling.

"Steffen is right. I'm one of the good guys," he said somberly, "but I know what you're planning to do, and I have to tell you—I don't think it's a good idea."

"What would *you* know about it?" snapped Maggie.

"I've seen it happen," Mr. Zoethout answered. "I've tried to warn folks myself, but people here haven't exactly warmed up to me. That's not important right now, though. What's important is that you four keep away from this thing. It's not safe! You'll only get yourselves hurt."

"Then what do we do about it?" asked Steffen. "What *is* the carousel? Who's behind it, and why do they want to take people from Widowsbury? We can't just ignore it. People are disappearing!"

"And getting eaten!" Beatrice interjected.

Maggie picked up a small pebble and tossed it at the carousel, where it bounced off and rolled back to her.

"I wouldn't want the people of Widowsbury if they were made of gold," she grumbled.

"I can't explain why it does what it does, but I have a theory about how to stop it," said Mr. Zoethout. "The thing is, I can't do it on my own. I'm gonna need at least two other people. Maybe more than that! But I don't have a lot of friends in town, so I'm afraid it's useless."

"You don't need friends. You've got us! Er, what I mean is . . . ," said Beatrice.

"What she means is, maybe we can help?" said Steffen.

"Nah, it's . . . it's stupid. I don't even know how I'd explain it," said Mr. Zoethout. He thought for a moment and then said, "Here! Give me your hand, and I'll show you!"

Before Adelaide could protest, Mr. Zoethout grabbed her hand, only to drop it just as quickly with a shout. A look of pain seized his face, and he turned away. Adelaide could see he was trembling.

"Mr. Z?" said Steffen.

Adelaide looked down at her hand, which looked normal to her. She smelled blood and saw droplets falling from Mr. Zoethout's lip where he had bitten it.

"N-no, it's much too d-dangerous!" he stuttered with his back to them. "Like I told you . . . I have to get more people. You're just . . . just children."

Steffen walked over to the candy man and tried to see his face.

"What's the matter, Mr. Z?" he asked, but Mr. Zoethout turned away yet again.

"Go! Now! Don't . . . stand there! I already told you it's not safe!" he yelled.

"I don't understand," Steffen said.

Adelaide grabbed his arm and pulled him along.

"We need to go. Right now," she warned. The bad feeling was even stronger now. Every part of Adelaide's bones said that something was very, very wrong right now.

"What was that all about?" asked Beatrice as they ran.

"I don't know, but I think it's more than he's telling us," said Adelaide.

They stopped to catch their breath, resting against the ancient swing set, which squealed in complaint. On top of it, a crow eyed them curiously.

Steffen said, "Hey, Adelaide."

"Yeah?"

"Anyone ever told you your ears are pointed?"

Adelaide drew back.

"*What* did you say?"

Beatrice and Maggie waved frantically for Steffen not to go any further, but he didn't see their warnings.

"Is it because you're a werewolf?" he asked innocently.

Adelaide glared. Her pupils dilated, and her nostrils flared.

"Steffen!" Beatrice whispered.

"It's okay if you are. I always wanted to meet one," Steffen went on. Suddenly Adelaide lunged, her hands at his collar. "Ow!" Steffen yelped.

"Adelaide, no!!" Beatrice cried. In a blink, Maggie leaped and yanked Adelaide off the boy.

"What did you do that for? I was only asking a question!" Steffen whined.

"Has anyone ever told you your clothes are patched or that you smell like peanut butter?" Adelaide growled. "Has anyone ever asked you why you don't go to school like the other boys? Is it because you're *poor*?"

Steffen's shoulders fell.

"You didn't have to say that," he said quietly.

"Don't you ever call me a werewolf again!" Adelaide threatened, her face flushed.

Steffen said nothing and looked down and away. Adelaide ran back toward Madame Gertrude's. Maggie groaned and took off after her.

"I'm sorry, Steffen! She didn't mean it, I promise," said Beatrice, and she, too, was gone, leaving Steffen alone in the park, wondering what in the world had just happened, and why everyone he came to like turned out to be crazy.

There was a welcoming committee awaiting the girls.

Mrs. Merryweather, the cook, Miss Patricia, and Steffen's father stood before the doors of Madame Gertrude's. They had flour and bits of dough all over their clothes and shoes and hair. And they most certainly were not smiling, although Mrs. Merryweather looked so livid that her scowl had almost gone full circle and turned upright again. There was no question as to what lay in store for the girls now.

"No, please, Mrs. Merryweather!" Beatrice begged. "Please!"

The entrance to the Wailing Room was a frightening affair of thick iron, multiple latches, and an array of rusty combination locks that hung about the heavy chains like ornaments of doom. It was not enough that the room was on the topmost floor of the school, nor that it lay at the end of a long, narrow corridor so that the dread could be drawn out as much as possible. It was also here that the lights had burnt out, leaving a halo of darkness. And worse—there were handprints on the outside of the door, where other students had desperately tried to get away. Ages of dust had gathered all around the oil left behind by sweaty palms and fingers.

"Baking soda in the vinegar tank, eh? Who taught you that? The cook's boy?" asked Miss Patricia as she held the struggling girls in place.

"That wasn't us! I swear!" Beatrice cried, but Mrs. Merryweather wasn't listening. It seemed like forever before she had unchained the door.

"Put them in," she ordered Miss Patricia, and though it took considerable effort even for Miss Patricia, she managed to deposit the prisoners.

"Guard the door!" commanded Mrs. Merryweather. She stood at the entrance and eyed the three girls with wrath so chilling that even the Blood Countess Báthory would have been shaken.

"You have done this to yourselves," she hissed at the cowering girls. "I have burnt out my last candle of patience on these stunts of yours! I warned you! I have been lenient until now, but you have torn apart my very last nerve! And so you will spend the rest of the day in this room. You will not have dinner. You will not partake of the Evening Hobby. You will stay here until the sun goes down, and even then I shall have to consider whether you're sufficiently sorry for the shame you have brought down upon this school's name!"

Adelaide rushed forward and collapsed to her knees.

"Mrs. Merryweather, you have to listen to us! Please—" she began.

"Quiet, little degenerates!" Mrs. Merryweather shouted. "I have made up my mind. You have forced me to take this measure, and so it is by force that you shall learn to behave in my school!

"It is a pity for you three," she added with a wry smile. "I have plans to take the whole school to the new carousel in Widowsbury Park. It opens this very afternoon! But not for you. The other girls have earned this privilege, and you would seek to ruin it for them!"

"*No!*" cried the girls.

"Mrs. Merryweather, if you take them there, something terrible will happen!" Adelaide pleaded. "Whoever is running that carousel is evil! And he's using it to—"

"I will not listen to threats!" Mrs. Merryweather thundered. "With that, I bid you good day, ladies. May you be protected from the darkness of your own souls! The rest of us are going to have *fun!*"

She left the room and gestured for Miss Patricia to seal it up. The door was shut. The latches slid closed and the twenty-odd locks clicked one at a time. Then there were no sounds but the girls' own breathing.

A man in a pink-and-white-striped apron was kneeling in the heart of the woods where no one could see him. Convulsing painfully, he spat out a string of curses at no one.

"Control yourself!" Mr. Zoethout ordered himself. But he could not. His body was rippling and warping, his lips bleeding as his teeth sharpened themselves before the rest of his face had caught up.

An avalanche of painful images and thoughts had crashed into his mind when he touched the wolf girl's hand. Her memories burned into his brain and exposed his own. He had always sensed something about the four children that made him intensely uncomfortable, but never had he felt it so keenly! In a flash, he had seen everything the girl experienced every day. Faces—cruel children's faces—laughing and mocking. Fingers pointing. He heard their insults and their songs. *Sca-ry chil-dren! Sca-ry chil-dren!*

He clutched at his head and tried to claw the thoughts out of himself, but he knew he could not. He saw the other freak children in the girl's mind. Sometimes they smiled kindly. Sometimes they looked at her with the same fear as the others. *Even they think I'm a freak. Just because I can hear and run and smell and . . . I'm not a werewolf!*

"Stop this!" Mr. Zoethout screamed. The faces in his head were turning into faces from his past. Faces he hated and swore he would destroy. He should have destroyed these other children, too. They made him weak, and just when he was so close! He could have taken them then, but something stayed his hand. Pity. Or empathy? Filthy words.

"Perhaps we can spare them?" he pleaded. His back jerked, and he held his sides to keep from twisting again. Another voice spoke inside his mind. It was gentle and calming. A warm, comforting wave.

But you must, it said. *They are stained by this town. We promised each other. You promised me.*

"Then what should I do?" wept Mr. Zoethout. "Tell me what to do!"

He heard no voices now. Only the crows in the barren trees mocking him. Trembling still, he smoothed back his hair and replaced his cap. He wiped the sweat from his pallid brow and took a few calming breaths.

I must remain calm. This emotion does not suit our purpose, he thought. *I will do away with those four when the time is right. For now, our work must continue.*

He strolled casually back into the park and to his candy stand. Already waiting there was an attractive young woman with rosy cheeks and delicate hands full of money.

"Oh, there you are!" she said reproachfully. "I was afraid I wouldn't be able to fill my sweet tooth today, Mr. Zoethout!"

"I'm awful sorry, miss," he said with a faltering voice. He

prepared the woman's usual order of chocolate coins and almond-crusted cream medallions.

The woman tilted her head and looked at him quizzically.

"Are you all right?" she asked, for she had noticed his red-rimmed eyes and the gleam of half-dried tears on his cheeks.

Mr. Zoethout hesitated and then laughed softly. "I'm fine. Don't you worry about me! It's all the mold," he said. He tapped his nose. "Gets to my allergies something awful."

"Yes, I know! Does it to me, too," said the woman. She took the chocolates and counted her money.

"Gosh, no! It's no charge," said Mr. Zoethout.

"Are you . . . sure?"

Mr. Zoethout took off his hat.

"If you insist on paying, I'll accept it in the form of accompanying me on a walk through the woods," he said. "I find it to be the only way to clear my stuffy head sometimes."

The woman blushed profusely. "That would be lovely!" she answered.

"*Wonderful,*" said Mr. Zoethout. He fished through his apron pocket and pulled out a smooth white pocket watch with funny-looking hands.

"It won't take long," he said. He checked the time and then slipped the watch back into his apron. He smiled a very wide and peculiar smile, his green eyes sparkling with flecks of yellow.

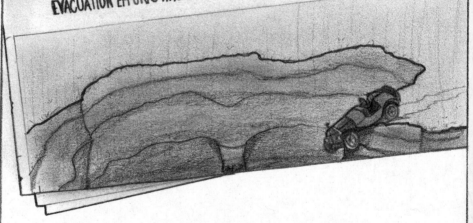

Widowsbury Herald

SPECIAL EDITION

DECEMBER 18, 1912

TWO CENTS

CURSED!

EVACUATION EFFORTS HALTED AS MASSIVE SINKHOLE SWALLOWS 150 AT BORDER

-Chapter Ten-
Betrayal

This was it. The end. Their lives were over. They stared at the heavily locked door in shock before the panic set in, and when it set in, it struck them all at once.

Maggie went to work on the door handle but to no avail. Adelaide ran from one wall to another and back again. She had no idea what she was searching for and could hardly see a thing as it was, but she couldn't bear to stand around.

Beatrice sank to her knees and covered her eyes. "I don't want to see! I'm not opening my eyes until Mrs. Merryweather comes back!" she sobbed.

"She's not *going* to come back, can't you see that?" Maggie snapped. She threw her weight into the door, but it was pointless.

"Don't yell at her like that! You're scared, too!" Adelaide shouted.

A small amount of light streamed in through a tiny dust-glazed window near the ceiling, she noticed, but that window was no bigger than a human head.

"Shut up! I'm not scared of a stupid legend!" Maggie yelled. A loose clump of plaster fell from the ceiling to the back of her neck, and she jumped.

"What was that?" she shrieked.

"I thought you weren't scared!" Adelaide taunted.

"I just don't like it when things sneak up on me, all right?" said Maggie.

"I want to go home!" Beatrice cried.

"Beatrice? Not. Helping."

"Oh, leave her alone, Maggie!"

"Look, I just need a second to think!"

"I want my daddy!"

It was the sound that interrupted their argument. A sound pulled up from the very depths of their darkest nightmares. It froze them to the bone, made every hair on their arms stand alert and the blood drain from their faces.

The wailing.

It started off low. Then it grew louder and more frantic—the keening of a spirit demanding repayment for its long-lost life. And they were trapped here with it.

Maggie and Adelaide dropped to the floor, eyes wide with terror. Beatrice's sobbing was hysterical now, and it didn't stop until she cried herself into a coughing fit.

"It's nothing. It's just a sound. It can't hurt us," said Adelaide, but her voice failed her.

"Yes it can! If it wants to, it can! Oh, I wish Phillip were here!" Beatrice cried.

"Why isn't he?" asked Adelaide.

"He got scared and ran away already!" Beatrice blubbered.

The wailing ended. How long it would rest they didn't know. They held their breath, waiting for the ghost to make its presence known once more, but it was quiet for now.

"It's gone. We're all right. It's okay," said Adelaide, more to reassure herself than anyone else.

"It'll come back . . . ," Beatrice sniffled.

"No it won't. I'll beat it up if it does. How's that?" said Maggie, but her show of bravery wasn't particularly convincing.

Adelaide allowed her eyes to adjust and studied the dim room once more. She refused to believe there was absolutely no way out. There were about two dozen school desks in the room, all bolted to the floor and covered in gray sheets of dust and cobwebs. A collection of carpentry tools and ladders stood haphazardly in a corner, and scattered across the floor was debris comprised of school papers and dried-up inkwells mixed with crumbs of yellowed chalk. She also noticed some suspicious dark stains, but she could not tell what color they were.

It's just old ink. That's all, Adelaide told herself, but she was having trouble believing this, particularly when she glanced up at the blackboard in the front of the room. Still written on it in ages-old chalk was a list of city names. The last one trailed off before the writer had finished spelling "Stockholm." On the floor just in front of the blackboard lay the legendary map whose heavy metal housing had once felled a teacher, if the legend was to be believed.

197

Another sound attracted Adelaide's attention, and she ran to the wall with the window, pressing her ear to it.

"What is it?" Maggie asked.

"People," said Adelaide. "I hear people walking and laughing. That's Miss Patricia! And Mrs. Paula! Oh no!"

"What?" Beatrice whined, still covering her eyes.

"They're going to the park now," said Adelaide.

"To the carousel," said Maggie.

Beatrice, still sniffling, crawled underneath a desk and rested her head and arms on the seat. "What are we going to do?" she cried. "How can we stop them now?"

Maggie thought, then moved swiftly to the collection of tools. She dragged a ladder away from the wall and positioned it under the tiny window.

"Adelaide, hand me some of that junk over there. I bet I can throw something at them!" she declared, and she climbed to the top of the ladder. With a hammer Adelaide pulled from the rubbish, Maggie wrenched the window frame away from the wall. She threw an inkwell. She tossed three chalkboard erasers. She even hurled the hammer. But everything she threw simply crashed down onto one of the gables below. All she could do was watch as her classmates and teachers streamed out of the building and up the road like ants into a trap.

"Never mind," she said. "It's hopeless. They're doomed, and so are we."

"I just don't understand. Why would they go there, anyway?"

Adelaide asked. "Merryweather hates that sort of thing! She's always said games and rides were for infants. It's like someone else was talking through her mouth!"

Maggie climbed down the ladder and angrily kicked it across the room. Then she took a deep breath and exhaled. As soon as the breath escaped her lips, the wailing sound started up again. She froze where she stood.

"Oh no . . . ," Beatrice mewled.

"Hush, Beatrice. Come on. We have to be brave right now," said Adelaide, even though she could scarcely keep her own wits together, let alone anyone else's.

"I can't be brave! I've heard them all my life, but I've never not been able to get away before!" Beatrice cried.

The wailing grew into an impatient yowl. Adelaide tried her hardest to at least sound brave even if she didn't particularly feel it. "I've learned that the best way to get rid of someone mean is to ignore them," she said in a hopeful voice. "I bet you it's the same way with ghosts!"

"It's not!"

"Please, Beatrice. I'm trying not to lose my head, all right?" Adelaide snapped, but Beatrice only cried harder.

"Can we talk about something else? You two are making me nervous!" said Maggie, her back pressed up against the wall.

"It's freezing in here!" Beatrice moaned. "It always gets cold when there's an Other Ghost nearby! They're the only ones who can change the temperature!"

"It also gets cold when the window's broken" Maggie hissed.

"All right, all right, all right! Let's not start fighting again!" said Adelaide. "Maggie's right. We should talk about something else. How about our parents? What do they do? Why did they come to Widowsbury? Where were you before this? Somebody just say something!"

As if it, too, wanted to listen, the ghost ceased its complaints. The room was still again.

Beatrice slowly raised her head and opened her eyes. They were red and puffy. "Bishop's Plot. I'm from Bishop's Plot," she said softly.

"Okay. That's a good start," said Adelaide. "What was Bishop's Plot like?"

Beatrice wiped her eyes with her arm and stared at the floor. "It was nice," she said, and she smiled a little.

"It's in the country. We had a big house with a pretty garden," she continued, "and a little cottage in the back where Daddy did the embalming and Mama did the makeup. They're morticians. I had school at home with my tutor. Her name was Miss Parish, and she lived with us. I liked her a lot, but I think I scared her away."

"Sounds familiar," said Maggie.

"How did you scare her away?" asked Adelaide.

"I didn't mean to," said Beatrice. "I've seen the animals all my life. The dead ones. I didn't know it was special until I started seeing the Other Ghosts, too."

"You mean people," Adelaide clarified.

"I mean ghosts that *used* to be people. They're not anything like people when they come back," said Beatrice. "They used to keep me up all night. Daddy rented out a warehouse and moved his embalming there just in case the cottage was where they were coming from, but it didn't help at all. At least Mama and Daddy believed me. Miss Parish thought I was making it all up. One day I saw an old man whom I'd seen in one of Miss Parish's photos. When I described him to her, she cried a lot. Then she went away, and I never saw her again. She never even wrote any letters."

A new tear trickled down her cheek.

"I had a lot of other tutors after that, but none of them stayed very long," she went on. "Then a lot of things changed. My parents got written about in a glamour magazine. I remember the article. It was called 'The Fashionable Dead of Bishop's Plot,' and it was all about how my parents made dead people look beautiful. They started getting requests from all over the world to embalm famous dead people. We traveled all the time! I was happy then. I didn't see the ghosts as much, though I missed my squirrels and mice dreadfully. Then Daddy said that all the travel and celebrity wasn't good for me, so they decided that I should live in a quiet town somewhere and go to a girls' school. And then I came here."

Beatrice heaved a heavy sigh.

"I miss them," she said. "Mama says they will try to write more, but they get so very busy with all the corpses."

A moth fluttered in through the open window and settled onto the rolled-up map, startling Adelaide and Maggie. Both wondered if perhaps this getting-to-know-you session was ill-advised. Suddenly, as if a switch was tripped, Beatrice smiled brightly.

"Maggie's turn!" she chirped.

Maggie looked away. She even blushed a little.

"Don't be proud," said Adelaide.

"I'm boring. Really. Not worth talking about," Maggie said.

"I like boring!" said Beatrice.

"Go ahead. Before that . . . thing starts going off again. Just talk about anything," Adelaide pleaded.

Maggie shrugged and sat down on the floor with the other two.

"Fine. If you really want to know," she said.

"We really want to know," Beatrice confirmed.

Maggie rolled her eyes. "It's not a big surprise, but my family's a bunch of circus freaks," she said. "My parents. My grandparents. Their parents. Freaks. All of 'em. My great-uncle Barrett was the World's Hairiest Man until he lost his title to somebody else in 1891, and he was mad about that for the rest of his life. My great-great-grandmother Cecilia was a fortune-teller. Made a lot of money until somebody called her a fraud because she wasn't seeing the future so much as making it happen."

"Wow," said Adelaide.

"I told you," said Maggie. "Bunch of freaks. Ma and Dad are strongmen. I mean, strongwoman and strongman. Ma gets upset if you don't say it right. My dad didn't want to go off to the circus. He wanted to be an accountant and be 'normal,' but Ma convinced him it was his calling after he stopped some bank robbers by throwing a safe at them. And when I say 'safe,' I mean one of the big ones you can stand up in."

"No! He didn't really do that, did he?" said Beatrice.

"Ma says he did," Maggie continued. "After that, they went off and joined the circus. But they thought it would be a good idea for me to grow up in a 'normal setting.' They wanted me to figure out on my own if I was a freak like them, so I'd have a chance to be like everybody else if I wanted to. Some joke that turned out to be."

"Was that the school you went to before you came here?" asked Adelaide.

"Yeah," Maggie answered, "and for the record, I wasn't expelled. I was 'encouraged to advance in a more suitable institution.'"

"What does that mean?" asked Beatrice.

Maggie laughed bitterly. "It means they didn't want me around, but I can't say they didn't try," she said. "At first, I was their special project. They wanted to make me fit in. It was 'Maggie, sit like this' and 'Maggie, walk like that' and 'You'd be so pretty if you'd just smile.' It was all fake. I did have one teacher I liked, though. *He* never treated me like I was some kind of science project. His name was Mr. Alvarez, and he taught history. But he also had this rare condition called narcoleptic volubilis."

"What in the world is that?" asked Beatrice.

Maggie drew her knees up to her chest and rested her chin on them.

"It means he sleep-roller-skated, and it could hit him at any time, not just at night," said Maggie. "One day he was talking about the Mongols and Attila the Hun, and I saw him start to strap on his skates. I knew he was about to nod off, but that wasn't anything new. We all figured he'd snap out of it before he got too far. He usually did. This time he didn't. And the thing is, the building was really old, so some of the floors were kind of slanted. He usually had this safety barricade to keep himself from rolling too far, but one of the janitors had moved it the night before. Next thing I knew, Mr. Alvarez was rolling at top speed right toward the window. I mean, you couldn't rig something so perfectly if you tried!"

"What happened then?" Adelaide asked.

She tried not to sound quite so eager, but this! This was the explanation she'd been waiting for since school started! She'd been too afraid to ask before.

"I went after him. Nobody else was gonna do it," said Maggie. "I caught him just as he went flying outside. He would've cracked like an egg if I hadn't. For the first and last time I can remember, everybody treated me like I was a hero."

For an instant, there was a glimmer of pride in Maggie's eyes. Then it flickered out just as quickly as it had come.

"Everybody except the headmaster and my other teachers," she said. "They said it was a nice thing I had done and they were very grateful, blah-blah-blah. But no 'normal child' would have been able to do what I did, and they were afraid that my 'display of abnormal ability' meant I was 'regressing.' They wrote to my parents about it. Told them I was welcome to stay but they didn't have much hope for me. So my parents got fed up with that school and took me away."

Adelaide remembered to breathe. "Forgive me for saying so, but thank you. I've always wanted to ask you about that," she said.

"Yes, but how did you end up here?" asked Beatrice. "My parents found a write-up in a travel magazine. It was an old one, I think. In a dentist's office."

"One of their circus friends told them about it," said Maggie. "Makes sense, I guess. I mean, it figures that another freak would know about Widowsbury, you know? They're still running around with the circus, but that's okay. They send me the flyers from all their stops, so I always know where they are."

They sat quietly, each one dreading a recurrence of the wailing. But what Adelaide dreaded almost as much was her turn in the history lessons.

"Well?" said Maggie. "I've blabbed my story. What about yours?"

"It's hard to explain," Adelaide said, knowing this would not dissuade them but figuring it worth the try.

"Oh, out with it, Adelaide. It's only fair," said Beatrice.

"I don't remember all that much, really," said Adelaide. But the others would have none of it.

"Okay. If it's my turn, it's my turn," she said reluctantly.

A dry leaf scritched as it blew across the wooden floor. The rafters of the old room creaked.

"We came here about two years ago," said Adelaide. "We moved from place to place for most of my life before that. I don't remember a time when we weren't running to catch a train or a boat. We're originally from a place called Bukovina, but I don't remember it. I think we had different names then, too. Back then, my parents were doctors. Not the kind you go to when you're sick, but the kind who research diseases, and they won all kinds of awards. My mom says life was good then, but again, it's all a blur to me. I just remember flashes of things from when I was small. Happy things like my dad swinging me through the air or the smell of my mom's cozonac bread. But I remember bad things, too. Lots of shouting and crying. And a fire. I remember hiding for weeks. I think we were all sick with something. It's . . . I don't know, it's all fuzzy. I'm probably not even remembering it right."

The shadows stretched long across the floor, creating an elongated square from the clouded sunset peering through the window. The ghost let out a shrill whistle but was quiet again. Listening.

"Go on, Adelaide," Beatrice said gently.

"I remember standing on the deck of a ship," said Adelaide. "I think we were leaving the country then. I was standing there with my arms out, and the moonlight felt amazing. I could smell and hear everything! Even the tiniest thing! I heard the wood creaking all the way down in the bottom of the ship. That's my last really happy memory. Then my dad came up and took me down to their room below, and I wasn't allowed to go up to the top anymore. I wasn't allowed to do much of anything after that. Like I said, we moved all the time. My parents were—are—completely paranoid. They gave up all they were respected for and started researching cures for diseases nobody'd ever heard of. That's what they're doing now. It's why they took me here. They wanted me to go to school away from the rest of the world, somewhere their reputations wouldn't affect me. They actually thought it would be *safer* for me here. Can you believe that?"

"Where are your parents now?" asked Beatrice.

"I don't know," said Adelaide. "Probably in some weird old village that doesn't even have a mailman. They said they'd be back for Christmas. I guess I'll hear from them then."

There were no sounds for a while. They felt better than they had when they were thrown into the room, but fear still gripped each one of them. And now their light was getting dim. Nightfall approached. No one had come to release them.

"Do you hear how quiet it is?" Adelaide whispered.

"Yes! It's wonderful!" said Beatrice.

"No. I mean any sounds at all," said Adelaide. She rested her head on the floor and listened. "There's nothing going on down there. No sounds. No new smells. They haven't come back yet."

"I told you," said Maggie. "They were doomed as soon as they left."

"This is bad," said Adelaide. "Really, really, *really* bad. It's not about us getting in trouble anymore. Everyone is gone. Maybe forever. Because I don't hear anyone outside, either!"

"*Anywhere?*" asked Maggie.

"What are we going to do?" Beatrice squeaked.

Just then the wailing started up again and the room itself shook.

A gust of wind intruded through the window, and Beatrice threw herself to the floor, covering her head.

"No! Not again!" she cried.

Maggie clung to one of the bolted desks until her knuckles turned white.

"I'd feel a whole lot better if that thing would shut up!" she complained.

But Adelaide stood up.

"Wait a minute . . . ," she said thoughtfully. She made one shaky step at a time toward the sound. "I can hear it!"

"So can I, and I want it to stop!" said Beatrice.

"No! No, listen!" said Adelaide. "I couldn't hear it before. I was too distracted! But I think . . . I think . . . !"

She bit her lip, squeezed her eyes shut, and then ran toward the wall that seemed to be hiding the ghost. She pressed her ear to it and tried to quiet the pounding of her heart.

"Please, please tell me I'm right," she said hopefully.

She felt along the moldy wallpaper, digging into it with her fingernails.

"Aha!" she said. She clawed at the wallpaper until she had torn enough off to reveal that the wall was not merely a wall. For in the wall were newer, brighter planks of wood that appeared more lazily nailed than the rest.

"Maggie! I need your help!" she said.

"Oh no you don't! You need to get away from that wall!" said Maggie.

Adelaide scowled back at her. "Don't tell me you're a chicken now. Come over here and help me pry off these boards!" she snapped.

"No, Maggie!" Beatrice begged. "Leave it alone!"

Maggie looked at Beatrice. Then at Adelaide. Finally, she gave in.

"If I get my face clawed off by a dead substitute teacher, you'd better apologize for calling me a chicken," she threatened, and with a small amount of effort, she wrenched a board out of the wall.

Adelaide continued to tear at the wallpaper, revealing more rotting and mildewed boards and several new ones, which Maggie yanked off one at a time.

"There!" said Adelaide when the last of the boards had been removed.

Behind the wallpaper and the planks was a door. From behind that, the wailing sound was even louder now, but Adelaide had stumbled upon a reason for courage.

"We have to open it," she said.

"Why are you doing this to us? You want us to die!" Beatrice sobbed.

"Beatrice, you're going to have to trust me," said Adelaide. She motioned to Maggie, who, despite her skepticism, barreled into the door and forced it open.

It was a closet, just big enough for three people to stand in. It had shelves on one side stuffed with books and papers and an inordinate number of cans containing insecticide powder and rat poison.

"It's just a closet full of junk," said Maggie with wonder, although she wasn't sure what else she had expected. A tomb full of expired students? Maybe. But she'd never admit to believing such things.

"Look at this!" said Adelaide.

She knelt down to the dusty floor, where she found a series of large pipes that ran along the baseboards and turned, ending in the back wall of the closet.

"Hey . . . ," Maggie said.

She stooped and twisted the largest pipe out of the wall to reveal that it was completely hollow and open at one end. And with a final, plaintive hoot, the wailing sound died for good.

"It was wind!" Adelaide said with a relieved laugh. "Beatrice! Come here! There's no ghost! Only the wind blowing through an open pipe! Oh, I feel so silly now."

Beatrice opened her eyes reluctantly and blinked.

"Promise?" she asked.

"*Yes!*" Adelaide and Maggie said at the same time. Beatrice crept warily over to the newfound closet and peered inside.

"I don't *see* any ghosts . . . ," she said uncertainly.

Maggie pounded on the back wall of the closet. "I think there's a window or something back here. I feel a draft between the boards," she said.

"Maggie, you're brilliant! If that's a window, we can use it to get outside!" Adelaide said excitedly.

Maggie struggled to remove a board and winced as she got a splinter in her palm. "Not so fast," she said. "Somebody took extra special care to board it up. It's going to take me a little time to pull all the planks off, and I don't know how big it is, or if we'll even be able to get down from there. So, just give me a minute to figure it out first."

"Go, Maggie, go!" Beatrice sang.

While she worked, Adelaide and Beatrice rifled through the stacks of old newspapers piled up inside. They went back as far as twelve years. The ones at the bottom had headlines like Plum Parade Goes Off Without a Hitch and Georgia Wilkes Crowned Miss Widowsbury 1912.

"It used to be so pretty," said Beatrice.

But the headlines took an increasingly macabre turn with each more current paper. Terrible Storm Strikes Widowsbury said another. Then its subhead: Weathermen Say No End in Sight. There was a period of days when there were no papers at all, and then a flurry of them, each reporting new horrors of monster attacks and unnatural accidents. Widowsbury School Vanishes said one article. Cursed! Evacuation Efforts Halted as Massive Sinkhole Swallows 150 at Border said another.

"Look at this one," said Adelaide, holding up a ragged front page dated nine years before.

"How did they have sea monsters without any sea?" asked Beatrice.

Then she squinted at the page and tore it from Adelaide's hand. "It's her! The ghost girl I've been telling you about!" she said excitedly. She held up the page and pointed to a small article at the bottom that featured a photograph of a teenage girl with perfect curls and dimpled cheeks.

DAUGHTER OF JUDGE VANISHES said the headline. MARGRET BELLHOUSE, 15, LAST SEEN IN THE COMPANY OF SCHOOLMATE. Below her photograph was another smaller one, this one showing a pimple-faced boy. Its caption said: *Nathan Wick, 15, also missing.* There was little information about the incident, only a lot of quotes from locals who had known the girl. There was next to nothing about the boy.

"If she disappeared nine years ago, that means...," said Adelaide. She put a hand to her mouth. "How long has this been happening?!"

Beatrice stared at the article again, held it at arm's length, then up close again.

"I've seen him before," she said, indicating the photograph of the boy.

"Maybe he turned up later, and you've seen him around," said Adelaide.

Beatrice shook her head. "No," she said. "I mean he looks like someone I know, but I'm not sure who. I don't know a lot of people."

Adelaide gave the paper a second look. "I guess he does look sort of familiar," she said.

With a shout of victory, Maggie succeeded in prying off the last of the boards, revealing a tall, broken window.

"Hooray for us!" said Adelaide.

"Hooray for Maggie!" Beatrice sang, clapping her hands.

Maggie kicked the rest of the glass from the window frame and stuck her head out into the cold evening air. It was very dark outside, and there was no moon. The sky was an ominous void.

"Boy, are we lucky!" she said, and she hopped out through the window. "There's a fire escape. Come on!"

The three girls climbed down the wobbly ladder and jumped one at a time to the ground. What they saw made their blood freeze. The streetlamps had not been lighted. Windows of neighboring buildings were black. Flyers advertising the fair fluttered wildly across the ground. The town, it appeared, had been deserted.

In the distance, they heard the lamentations of a calliope. The tune it played was a funeral dirge, and Adelaide realized with a deepening dread that it was the same tune the shadowy man had been humming the night before. She strained to listen for possible evidence of other people, but there was nothing. She heard only the calliope, the brushing of tree limbs in the breeze, and the breathing of her companions. But then she remembered someone.

"Steffen!" she cried. "He wouldn't have gone to the carousel of his own will! He might still be here!"

"Oh, I hope he hasn't gotten eaten!" said Beatrice.

"Then we'd better hurry," said Maggie, and the three of them rushed across the street to the dark steps of Rudyard School.

All its windows were dark except for one near the ground, which glowed with candlelight. They peeked inside, where they saw their fair-headed friend. He was scurrying about his room, shoving various odd items—tin cans, balls of string, part of what looked like a harpoon—into his knapsack.

Beatrice rapped on the glass with her knuckles, startling him. Then he raced to the window and unlatched it with a laugh of relief.

"I was sure you three were lost with the others! I was afraid I'd have to go out there alone!" he said.

"Not a chance!" said Beatrice. "We're not allowed to go anywhere! Not even to our own deaths!"

Steffen looked at Adelaide and then down at his feet.

"Hey, Adelaide," he said shyly.

"Hey, Steffen," said Adelaide. She scratched her arm nervously.

"Are we going to stand around saying 'howdy' to each other, or are we going to find out what's happened?" Maggie griped.

"Right. Sorry," said Steffen. He was about to climb out through the window when he stopped and jumped back down.

"What is it now?" Maggie groaned.

"I'll be right there!" said the boy. "I've got to get some more sandwiches! Dad would be so mad if I didn't have any!"

"Your dad's already . . . I mean, he's . . . well, hurry up!" Maggie said impatiently. She had to remind herself that it wasn't her father in the belly of a monster, and some occasions required a little sensitivity.

Steffen returned moments later, his knapsack crammed with so much food and miscellaneous junk that he experienced some difficulty climbing out the window.

"Why didn't you just use your door?" asked Maggie. "What is it with everyone and doors, anyway?"

"It's locked," said Steffen sheepishly. "I'm sort of grounded."

"I won't say a word," Beatrice promised.

The four of them ran for the park, low thunder rumbling in accompaniment with the carousel's sad calliope. When they reached the park, they kept to the shadows and the trees, moving slowly and cautiously to avoid being seen. By what they could not guess. But it was evil and not bound by the laws of nature, and it was generally a good idea to stay out of such things' line of sight. It was right about now that Adelaide desperately wished they had Steffen's unpatented invisibility helmet. And, of course, that it worked.

They stopped before they came to the clearing where the carousel stood—a massive, towering cage of prancing unicorns and galloping horses. It had grown. It was positively enormous—easily four times the size it had been only hours earlier. Its canopy bulged awkwardly at the peak. Where once there had been single portraits in each pane there were now scenes containing hundreds of people.

"I think I see Mrs. Merryweather in there!" said Adelaide.

"It's like the thing has gotten fat off everyone we know!" said Steffen.

"Hold on . . . ," said Adelaide. Somewhere beyond the mournful calliope music, she heard someone sniffling.

"We're not alone," she said in a low voice. She tiptoed back down the crooked path and through the trees. The others followed closely behind as the crying sound led Adelaide to the now-broken and, by all appearances, abandoned Candy Time stand.

"What happened here?" said Adelaide. The sign over the stand had been hacked to shreds. The fake clock with its too few numbers had red paint splashed all over it. On the ground before the stand, the cash register lay in pieces.

The crying and sniffling was louder now. Adelaide stepped quietly toward the stand and looked behind it, where she found a man in a striped apron curled up below the counter.

"Mr. Zoethout!" she said, surprised.

"What's happened? Is he all right?" asked Beatrice.

Mr. Zoethout covered his face with his hands and shook his head stubbornly. "Leave me alone!" he yelled.

"It's all right, Mr. Z. It's just us," said Steffen.

"Go away, I said!" Mr. Zoethout repeated. "You don't know what I've done!"

Adelaide drew back immediately. "What have you done, Mr. Zoethout?" she asked.

"You don't know what I've done, and you don't know who I am!" cried the candy man.

Beatrice left her place of safety with the others and walked over to the wrecked stand.

"Beatrice!" Maggie hissed in warning, but Beatrice ignored her. She stood at Mr. Zoethout's side and watched him for some time.

Finally, she said, "I know who you are."

"No. No, you don't!" Mr. Zoethout wept.

"Your name is Nathan, isn't it? Nathan Wick," said Beatrice.

The candy man looked up at her, confusion in his reddened eyes.

"How . . . ?" he questioned.

"You've got something to do with that carousel. I saw your picture in an old paper. You were younger then," Beatrice answered.

"Beatrice, get back! I have a very bad feeling right now!" Adelaide growled.

The man once known as Lyle Zoethout rose slowly to his feet. He was taller than they remembered, and his once-kindly face now seemed sharper somehow. Crueler.

"I don't know how you've made that connection, but it doesn't matter anymore," he said angrily. "It's all over now. It's gone too far. It's unstoppable!"

He turned and marched toward the woods. Adelaide charged after him with the others close behind. "What do you mean?" she demanded. "If the carousel is somehow your doing, I'll . . ."

But she honestly had no idea what she would do. This was all much bigger than she had imagined.

"Don't you see it?" Nathan cried. His eyes, once emerald green, were an odd lemony yellow. "I *am* the carousel!"

"Huh?" said Maggie.

"The carousel is me, and I am it!" said Nathan. Before them, the carousel loomed. "It is a creature that has become as dear to me as my own self. It is . . . it was my only friend!"

"You've got poor taste in friends, mister," said Adelaide.

"And who was I supposed to turn to?" Nathan shouted. "This town? I had no one! Everyone hated me. Everyone treated me like an inferior! But the creature was different. The creature understood me!"

"What are you talking about? What creature?" asked Steffen.

Nathan glared furiously at the boy.

"I see there is only one way you're ever going to understand," he said, and then he began to grow. He stretched up and up, growing tall and long as a shadow does, his yellow eyes afire.

"What are you?" Adelaide murmured.

Nathan ignored her, and pointed at the carousel and commanded it: "Show them!"

Bright green lightning burst from the earth and strangled the clouds, and the wind lashed at them.

"*Yesssssss . . . ,*" it breathed.

The children clung to each other and hid their faces from flying dust. Just when they were sure they could take this no longer, the wind dissolved into a single breath and was gone. The thunder and lightning died, and the cold night was replaced by warm sunshine.

Adelaide opened her eyes and saw that everything was completely different. There was no carousel. No Nathan Wick. Above her, she heard the delicate songs of sparrows and robins, and the skies were actually blue. She looked around for her friends, but she was alone, sitting on the sagging porch steps of a house she'd never seen.

"Nathan! Nathan Bartholomew!" a woman screeched inside the house. The woman—a tall and sickly-looking figure in old-fashioned clothing—stomped outside and glared at Adelaide.

"What do you think you're doing out here? You're a very sick boy!" she scolded, and then Adelaide understood. She was seeing Nathan Wick's memories through his own eyes.

"You know how the sunlight affects you," said the woman, who must have been Nathan's mother, "and I don't want you sneaking off to play with the children from town! They'll only make you worse. Yes, it's best if you stay right here with Father and me."

"But Father goes outside," said a boy through Adelaide's lips. "He goes into town every day!"

"Father must go to work, and *he* isn't a sick little boy!" snapped Mother.

"I don't feel sick. Why are you always telling me I am?" said Nathan, and Adelaide pulsed with frustration right along with him.

Everything raced before Adelaide's eyes as she felt herself propelled through time. She stood inside the house now, and from a dirty window she watched the sky turn pitch black as swiftly as if someone were painting over it. Evil storm clouds cloaked the valley in darkness. Rain splashed to the ground. Trees were broken and thrown all around the house. In the distance grew smoke from fires, and terrifying shadows crept in and out of the ground, all at the abnormal speed of Nathan's racing memories.

The Big Storm.

Time slowed down, and again Adelaide found herself sitting on the porch, staring down at something in the dirt near the base of the steps. The thing in question looked like nothing more than a clear blob of gelatin. With Adelaide's legs, Nathan moved quietly down the steps and poked at the blob on the ground. It wobbled when he touched it. Then a tiny tendril formed a finger and poked him right back. He laughed and then covered his mouth. *Mustn't be heard! Mother will bring me back inside!* Adelaide heard inside her head.

The mass on the ground began to grow and change, until it took the shape of a kitten, and Adelaide somehow knew that this was just the thing for which Nathan had been wishing. The creature, she realized, had read the boy's thoughts and changed shape to become his desire.

Soon Nathan's thoughts were replaced with the warm and soothing voice of the creature, speaking to him only in his mind.

I have been carried here by the winds and the rains, and I am lost and hungry, it said. *Feed me your sorrow, and I will return joy to you. Do this for me, and I will make you my master.*

Time rushed forward again, and Adelaide watched as Nathan returned to the sadness-eating creature time after time. Sometimes it was a cat. Sometimes a dog. Once, it even took the shape of a small biplane and flew Nathan around the yard, then up to his bedroom window before Mother walked outside to look for him. As it fed off Nathan's sadness, it became whatever he wanted, changing that sorrow into joy. Nathan loved the shape-changing creature,

and it seemed to love him, too. And as Mother allowed Nathan no human companions, it became his only friend.

Then came the dark times.

Nathan's house was destroyed by fire in a lightning storm. Only he and his creature escaped alive. Suddenly the boy who had never known another child in his life found himself forced to live among dozens of them at the Pernicious Valley Home for Orphans.

He didn't play the way the others did. His clothes were funny and outdated. He spoke too formally, and he cried all the time. Try as he might, he simply could not adapt, and the others taunted him mercilessly for it. Only the creature showed him any kindness. Nathan would beg it to avenge him, but it would always remind him gently: *No, master. I must only consume pain. Creating it would destroy everything good in me. But I promise I shall never leave you.* It remained true to its word.

The vision changed again, and Adelaide had the sense that Nathan was older in these memories, and he had fallen desperately in love with a girl from town. She had pretty brown hair, perfect dimpled cheeks, and eyes as blue as the sky was before the Storm. To Nathan, she seemed like an angel on earth, and her name was Margret Bellhouse.

Margret was as kind as she was pretty. She never seemed to mind Nathan's unpopularity, nor was she too proud to be seen with him. Her friends laughed at him all the time, but she refused to take part. Nathan was smitten, and he forgot all about the creature.

Sometimes Margret and Nathan went for evening walks together and talked of their favorite things. He learned that Margret loved horses, dreamed of being a theater actress, and longed to escape from Widowsbury, though her aunt and uncle had died attempting to do the same. She also loved carnivals and, while she admitted she was too old to ride one, she still adored the pretty carousels.

Then Nathan remembered his companion.

Adelaide watched as Nathan brought Margret into the woods one night. He covered her eyes and walked her over to his hiding place, where there now stood a carousel just big enough for two people to ride. It was an ugly thing, unlike any carousel Adelaide had ever seen. It had a dome like those on the churches in Russia. There were paintings of battle scenes on its panels. The horses resembled the kind she had seen in statues of famous war generals.

Nathan helped Margret up its wooden steps and then uncovered her eyes.

She sneered.

"What is this?" she asked.

"Why, it's a carousel," said Nathan. "You said you liked them. I made it for you because I love you, Margret Bellhouse!"

But Margret showed no joy at this news.

"Oh my," she said softly. "I had no idea you felt like that. If I'd known, I would have been more careful—"

"What do you mean?" Nathan interrupted.

223

"Please understand, Nathan," said Margret stiffly. "I hated to see you treated so cruelly and I'm happy to be your friend, but that's all. I just . . . well, I don't have those feelings for you."

For you. It was something about the way she said those two words that wounded Nathan more than anything ever had. Adelaide could feel the rage boiling up inside him. It had been boiling his whole life, but this rejection after so many was enough to send a lifetime of hurt and anger spilling right over.

"You think you're better than me, don't you?" Nathan seethed.

Margret took a nervous step away from him. "Now, Nathan, I didn't say that!" she insisted.

"But you're not denying it," spat Nathan. "Admit it! You only pretended you cared about me so you could laugh at me just like the rest of them!"

At this, he turned and stormed away, leaving Margret quite

alone on the carousel. His head, and Adelaide's, absolutely burned with the blackest of thoughts. The vile sort that no one ever admits to thinking.

Meanwhile, the creature was overwhelmed. Too long had its master neglected it, and now it had been asked to perform an extravagant transformation. All these violent feelings from Nathan flooded it—poisoning the creature, and mutating it into something too terrible to behold.

Margret screamed at the horrors forming around her. The carousel's horses were melting into misshapen, spitting masses. Their legs kicked madly in the evil muck. Margret tried to run, but her ankles were caught by a phantom hand that stretched up from the shifting floor and dragged her down into it.

"Nathan! Help me!" she shrieked.

But Nathan never looked back. The creature soon swallowed Margret up forever. All that remained was an echo of her final scream.

Adelaide knew as if she had seen this all before that the creature was changed forever. It had done the thing it should never do, and now it was injured beyond repair. Stuck in the shape of a carousel forever, it no longer responded simply to sadness. Now it required life itself for food, extracting it slowly and as horribly as possible.

The realm of Nathan's memories grew faint until it was nothing but mist that drifted away before Adelaide's eyes. Now she lay dazed in the mud of Henbane Wood. It had begun to rain. Beside her, Steffen, Maggie, and Beatrice blinked away their similar trances.

"I'm so sorry" was all Adelaide could think to say.

But now Nathan was sobbing horribly.

"I didn't know it would come to this," he wept. "I didn't know its hunger would become so voracious! Oh, for a time, I relished it! I wanted my revenge! I hid out in the woods with my dearest monster . . . plotting with it, growing with it, feeding from it until we were almost the same! I dreamed I would grow up, wait for this wretched town to forget me, and then return with another name and a new purpose. For who would suspect such a sweet and charming candy man of luring his old enemies to their doom with his innocent little treats?"

"The candy!" said Steffen.

"Created with the blood of the creature itself!" Nathan declared. "The very blood that has made me what I am is a poison in its concentrated form. How I loved watching you all devour it and answer its call. I particularly looked forward to watching all the schoolchildren march to me in one helpless herd! But now that it has happened, I cannot bear it! I am even worse than my tormentors now. I never wanted to become this. I beg you to forgive me. I've done a terrible thing!"

He fell to his knees dramatically, and his weeping surged. The rain wept along with him.

"Look. If anyone understands how you feel, it's us," said Adelaide as she fought to stand in the clinging mud, "but crying about it isn't going to help anyone. You have to stop that monster before it kills everyone! You're the only one who can help us!"

Nathan sniffed and stared at the children. "But why?" he asked them. "Why do you care about these people when they've made you suffer, too?"

His words inspired an ache in Adelaide's heart. He was right. Why did she care? *Just let them go. It would be easier*, said a voice inside her head, but that voice was not her own.

"What kind of people would we be if we let them all die a horrible death? Would that really make us any better?" asked Beatrice. "You said it yourself, Nathan Wick. You're worse than all of them now. And we do have a friend. She was eaten by *your* friend, and we want her back!"

The others agreed with enthusiasm.

Nathan dabbed at his eyes with the edge of his already soaked apron. "How *lucky* for you," he muttered. "Then I suppose we must do what must be done. It is too late even for me to stop it, but your people can be saved. And you must hurry or I will not be able to help you!"

"What do we do?" asked Steffen.

"You must enter the creature's belly and push its prey to freedom. It slumbers now, but I can awaken it for you," said Nathan. "But you must all go at once! You don't know what horrors await you there! One of you—even three of you is not enough to fight it! Tie yourselves together well. Young Steffen, I believe you have the tools? I will stay behind and pull you back. I am the only one who can. Hurry! There's not much time!" he ordered.

Steffen quickly fished through his knapsack and pulled out the rope. Then he and the girls tied themselves together as planned.

Maggie stood in front with Adelaide behind her. Next was Beatrice, with Steffen at the back.

"Now, give me the rope while there's still a chance!" Nathan demanded.

Steffen gingerly handed the loose end to Nathan. "You'd better not let us down," he said. "I would've been your friend, you know. I might still be your friend if you make this right, but I can't make any promises."

"Thank you, dear boy," said Nathan with a sorrowful smile.

"Steffen, before we do this, I just wanted to say I'm sorry for what I said to you earlier today. I didn't mean it," said Adelaide.

"'S all right," said Steffen with a short nod.

Adelaide returned his nod and then checked all her knots to make sure they were secure.

"Nathan?" she called.

Nathan tugged on the rope to show he held it tightly.

"Let's go," said Adelaide. Then the four of them ran forward in a row and jumped onto the carousel's platform. They waited.

Down on the ground, Nathan closed his eyes and stretched out his arms, gripping the rope in one hand.

"Wake up, my friend! I bring new gifts for you! Wake up, I tell you!"

Overhead, thunder crackled and wind swirled around the children. The carousel began to revolve. With each turn, the scenery around them blurred a little more, the trees and Nathan turning into nothing more than smears of ink in the flashes of lightning. They could not even feel the rain.

"Oh, Adelaide, I don't like this!" shouted Beatrice.

Adelaide reached back and squeezed her hand.

"We can do this! It's the only way!" she shouted.

The carousel was spinning faster now—faster than the scariest rides at carnivals ever went.

"Why do I have the feeling we're going to regret this?" asked Maggie.

"I'd be more worried if you didn't! Is everyone all right so far?" Adelaide asked.

"I'm getting dizzy, but I'll make it!" Beatrice squeaked.

"I hate this!" Maggie yelled.

But Steffen didn't say anything.

"Steffen?" Adelaide called again.

"We've got a little problem," he finally replied, and he held up the end of the rope. The end Nathan was supposed to be holding.

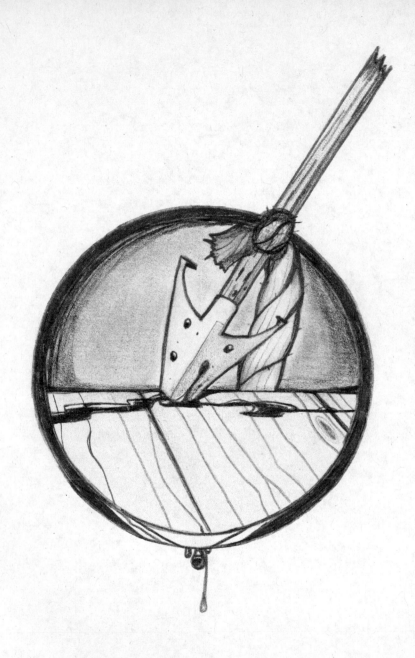

- Chapter Eleven -
A Terrible Spinning

The girls and Steffen were in a heap of trouble. Of this, there could be no question. Nor was there any question that they were spinning faster than they had ever spun in their lives, that the carousel that spun them was not of this world, and that if they did not find a way out of this predicament, they were as good as dead. But finding a way out would be most difficult. Even were it not for the force of the spinning that kept them clinging to the center column, the nausea alone was enough to put any ideas of escape right out of their dizzy heads.

"I knew he was lying! I knew it! You got any other bright ideas, Weller?" Maggie shouted to Steffen as she gritted her teeth against the sick feeling.

"Um . . . no! Sorry!" he answered.

Adelaide squeezed her eyes shut and tried to think about nicer things. Mostly things that didn't move. Even through the veil of her eyelids she could make out the bobbing motion of the carousel horses. Up and down and then up again—a monstrous jaw working

231

at its food. What a terrible realization it was that she and her friends were indeed that food! And there was nothing they could do about it except stand there and be digested.

Beatrice screamed.

"It's changing!" she shrieked, her voice carried away by the roar of the machinery and its ghastly calliope music.

Adelaide forced her eyes open. The carousel was rather dark, but in the dim crimson glow she could tell that the horses *were* changing. They twisted like snakes, very much alive, and their heads snapped side to side as their jaws cracked open. A strange red light beamed from their eyeless sockets, and they bared their jagged teeth with menace.

"Oh my God . . . ," Adelaide whispered.

The horses weren't the only monsters on this ride. Shadows welled up from the floor and took the shape of myriad other horrors. Spiders with rat heads. Rabid dogs with bat wings. They weaved in and out of solidity, oozing closer to the children with each transformation.

"What are they?" Maggie yelled.

"The poor dears," said Beatrice in a voice full of pity.

"What do you mean 'poor dears'?" Adelaide cried. "They're trying to kill us!"

"I can hear them in my head! They're ghosts of creatures the carousel has eaten before," Beatrice answered. "It's mixing them up—controlling them. It doesn't want us to leave!"

"Of course it doesn't! We're dinner!" Maggie shouted. Then, surprisingly, she yawned.

Adelaide tried to move but each effort felt as if a ten-pound weight had been added to her. She was exhausted. Worn out. Sapped and getting weaker. Beside her, Beatrice was already nodding off.

"I'm so . . . tired all of a sudden," yawned Adelaide. "What's going on?"

"We can't sleep! That's what it wants us to do!" Steffen shouted.

With effort deserving of a medal, he reached behind him into his knapsack and pulled out a bag of sandwiches. He stretched his arm over to shake Beatrice awake.

"Eat these!" he yelled.

"But I feel sick and sleepy!" whined Beatrice.

"How can you . . . possibly . . . think of food?" Adelaide asked drowsily. Her eyelids refused to lift themselves anymore.

"You have to!" said Steffen through a mouthful of peanut butter. "Something's sucking out all our strength! I know it's not much, but food might help! Hurry!"

"I don't want to!" Beatrice whimpered sleepily, but she reached back and took the sandwiches all the same. Reluctantly she ate a bite and passed the rest of the sandwiches to Adelaide and Maggie. And it worked. No sooner had they gotten a few bites down than they felt almost normal again. If "normal" could be defined as terrified, with a touch of vertigo. But the feeling lasted only briefly before exhaustion would creep up on them once more.

"We have to keep eating if we want to stay awake!" Steffen urged.

"How many of those have you got?" Adelaide asked.

"Something like twenty, but a few of them might be a little moldy," Steffen answered.

"Ew! Steffen!" Beatrice gagged.

The menagerie of shadow creatures melded into one giant black bear, which roared and made the whole carousel quake.

"Oh dear! We're making it angry!" Beatrice warned.

"Good!" said Maggie. "That means we're a threat to it. If it's afraid of a bunch of skinny kids like us, it must think we can beat it."

"What are you planning to do?" asked Adelaide, wincing as some unidentified debris whizzed past her cheek.

"We can't just stand here eating peanut butter sandwiches!" reasoned Maggie. "We're trapped in this thing! We may as well do something, and there's no reason we can't still do what we were going to do!"

She reeled a little but steadied herself with the help of the center column.

"Ugh," she groaned. "I'm awful dizzy, but I think I can still push people out of here. Miss Delia was able to help Henry, and I'm prob'ly a lot tougher than she was!"

"But how will *we* be rescued?" asked Beatrice.

The shadow bear roared again, but Maggie ignored it. "We'll cross that bridge when we come to it!" she said. "Now, if I could just see where I'm going!"

Steffen shouted something, but it sounded like muffled gibberish.

"Sorry!" he said, and he swallowed a bite of sandwich. "I said I can help with that!" He ducked to sort through his knapsack just as a shadowy claw swiped at the spot where his head used to be.

"Oh, Steffen, be careful!" Beatrice cried.

Steffen popped up with a helmet in his hands. How he managed to fit so much into one knapsack was anyone's guess. This particular helmet was built out of a steel colander, various wires, and two lightbulbs encased in metal tumblers that were strapped to the top with burlap strips.

"Headlights!" he announced with a grin.

"You found your lightbulbs!" said Adelaide gladly.

As soon as Steffen put the helmet on, the bulbs flickered to life brightly. Two small streams of light beamed in whichever direction Steffen chose to look. And the terrors they revealed were more horrible than any of the children had imagined.

Something else was happening.

"Look at them!" Beatrice shouted, pointing to the shadowy creatures. They were hissing and snapping even more viciously than before, but they also appeared to be backing away.

"They come from the dark! They don't like the light! Steffen, you're a genius!" Beatrice cheered.

"I am . . . ," Steffen murmured, amazed by his accidental weapon. But now something was slithering up behind him.

"Steffen! Quick! Turn around!" Adelaide shrieked.

Steffen whirled around, quick as a whip, which sent the biggest, blackest scorpion he'd ever seen in his life scrambling for darkness.

"Whoa! That was close!" he said.

The carousel quaked again in its rage, sending deep cracks up one side of the center column. Wounded, its spinning began to slow.

"You got any more of those headlight things?" asked Maggie.

"Afraid not!" answered Steffen. "Looks like you're just going to have to see as best as you can. I'll give you light when I'm able, but I've got to keep the monsters away!"

"Well, then we'd better get a move on!" shouted Maggie. "All the peanut butter sandwiches in the world aren't gonna keep me from losing my lunch before long!"

Adelaide heard a groan just ahead of them, and when she squinted into the fog, she made out the shape of a body.

"There!" she cried. "I found our first rescue! Steffen! Light, please?"

"Can't right now! Trust me on that!" Steffen called back amid what sounded like a swarm of angry hornets.

"Never mind. Just tell me what to look for, Adelaide!" Maggie shouted.

"I think he's to your left up ahead! On the floor! It sounds like a little boy!" Adelaide answered.

Maggie saw the boylike heap lying a few feet ahead, but when she reached him, he sprang from the floor and changed into something that was not human at all. It still looked like a boy, but it had three different mouths on its face, each lashing at her with a different forked tongue.

"Not a boy!" she yelled.

"It's a ghost monster!" Beatrice shouted. "I can feel him in my head like the others! The carousel's trying to trick us!"

The boyish thing lunged at them, but Steffen and his lights were quicker.

"Good job, Steffen!" said Adelaide. "Beatrice, can you identify other ghosts? I can't tell the difference until it's too late!"

"I'll try!" Beatrice promised through a wad of sandwich.

"Good, because I can smell someone now!" said Adelaide. "Maggie! To our left! Against the column!"

Maggie felt around in the vaguely reddish darkness until her hands landed on fabric. It was something that felt like overalls. In the glow, she thought she recognized a familiar bald head.

"It looks like Elmer Whitley!" she called out.

"He's real!" Beatrice confirmed.

Maggie hoisted the unconscious handyman over her shoulder and with a barbarian yell, heaved him into the outside world.

"Don't hurt them!" Beatrice cried.

"Can't promise you that," said Maggie. "I just get 'em out of here!"

Adelaide listened. "Right ahead of you!" she called out. "A young girl."

"Ghost!" Beatrice warned, and the girl turned into a child-sized tarantula that reared up on its back legs when Steffen spun toward it. It screamed in the light and melted into the floor, only to resurface as another creature somewhere else.

The hunt, it seemed, went on forever as Maggie tugged them forward while Adelaide and Beatrice identified other victims.

"There's a man over there! I hear him breathing!"

"No you don't! It's a ghost!"

237

"Look! Miss Patricia! Over here!"

"Real! Unfortunately."

On and on they searched. Steffen kept at the rear, warding off monsters with his headlights until the maniacal zoo had gotten so crowded he could look in one spot barely more than a second. All the while, the calliope desperately blared.

"If we ever make it out of this alive, I'm never eating another peanut butter sandwich as long as I live," Maggie groused as she rolled a particularly hefty man off the platform.

"Agreed!" said Adelaide, who was doing her best to fight off the urge to gag. "How are we doing, Maggie? I can't tell how far we've gone! And my head hurts!"

Maggie ducked a shadow serpent that dropped toward her from above.

"Looks like we're done with this level!" she yelled back.

"What do you mean *this level?*" asked Steffen. "There's more?"

Maggie tugged on the rope, yanking the others closer, and pointed down. In the center of the floor, where part of the column had at last given way, was a deep, round chasm with what looked like dozens of other levels just like theirs.

"Oh no," Beatrice moaned. "How are we ever going to get down there?"

"And even if we do, we can't get all those people out by ourselves! There's only four of us!" Adelaide cried.

"Wait!" Steffen exclaimed. "I've got something in my bag still!"

He braced his feet to keep from falling and retrieved his harpoon spear.

"Help me untie myself, Maggie!" he called.

Adelaide grabbed on to his arms. "What are you doing?! We'll get separated!" she yelled.

"I have a way to get you down there, but the rope won't hold with my extra weight!" he explained.

Steffen turned his helmet around to protect their backs while he loosened his end of the rope. He attached it to the harpoon and then swung the spear high above his head before plunging it down into the floor, where it stuck. The carousel shook violently in response, and the spinning slowed again.

"Okay! Jump!" Steffen ordered.

"What about you?" asked Beatrice.

"I'll stay up here and throw the spear back down to you. We'll need it again later!" he answered.

"I can catch you if you're not too scared to jump!" Maggie offered before she grabbed the rope and swung down with the others in tow. They made it just two feet short of the floor, all of them moaning with nausea. But Maggie wouldn't let that get in her way, and she signaled for Steffen to let them loose. He untied the rope and tore the spear from the floor, ignoring the painful shrieks emitted by the many shadow monsters. Then he tossed it down to the girls.

"Your turn!" Maggie yelled. "Jump!"

But Steffen hesitated, clinging to the jagged edges of the crumbling center column. The distance looked so much farther, now that he wasn't tethered to the others. The monsters at his sides looked so much closer, and he could only shine his light in one direction at a time. They seemed to know what he was thinking—daring him to challenge them.

"I—I—I'm not sure anymore!" he said. He felt ashamed of his fear, and he couldn't move his feet. The rapid revolutions of the carousel were getting to him now, and he felt his knees give out.

"Steffen!" the girls screamed below.

"I'm trying!" he said. He heard his father's voice in his head. *Just one foot at a time. Come on, Steffen. You didn't pack enough sandwiches. That's the problem.*

"RrrrAAAAAAAAAAA!!" he yowled, and finally he let go of the column.

But he was too slow. A great black flying lizard swooped up, enveloping him in its scaly wings. His glasses and helmet went tumbling down and smashed far below. Then the lizard darted down to another level, out of sight.

Beatrice screamed, "No!"

"Steffen?" Adelaide cried.

Maggie almost lost her footing. She stared up in disbelief at the empty space where Steffen had stood only seconds ago.

They called his name over and over, but the shadow monsters mimicked his voice now. Neither Adelaide nor Beatrice could tell which was real. There were too many.

"We have to keep going," Maggie said at last. "We can't find him on our own. We need to get out of here somehow and get more help."

"It got Steffen!" Beatrice sobbed. "We can't do it without Steffen! It has to be the four of us!"

Adelaide felt overwhelmed with weariness now. Tears stung her eyes, blurring her vision even more.

"Maggie's right. We have to keep moving. I'm sorry, Beatrice, but if the carousel gets us, *nobody* can help Steffen," she said. Her throat tightened, and her chest hurt.

I'm sorry, Steffen, she thought remorsefully. *I got you involved in this. It's my fault. I just hope you're still here somewhere. Please, Steffen, be alive!*

Beatrice would not be consoled. She balled up her fists at her sides. The black orbs of her eyes grew large, and her expression darkened into something so wrathful, so full of unbridled fury, that Maggie and Adelaide found themselves afraid of their own friend.

"Listen to me!!" Beatrice screamed. Her voice carried throughout all the levels of the carousel, echoing even amid the roaring chaos around them.

"Beatrice?" Adelaide whispered, but Beatrice was not speaking to Adelaide or Maggie. In fact, it didn't seem that it was Beatrice speaking at all but some other person inside Beatrice's tiny frame.

"Bring back my friend!" she commanded.

The shadow creatures crept backward, gnashing their shadowy teeth. The calliope music abruptly ended on a discordant chord.

Beatrice bowed her head, closed her eyes, and bellowed.

"If you won't tell me what you've done with my friend, you will leave us alone and go back to the dark and scary place!"

She opened her eyes again, and the shadow creatures shrieked all at once. They twisted and contorted, melding into one another until they formed one giant wolf that threw its head back and howled. Then it exploded into a confetti of black dusty particles and was gone. The carousel continued to turn but ever so slowly. Its mutating horse-monsters dried up and crumbled as paper does in a fire. The girls were alone inside the creature's belly.

"They . . . they listened to you. How did you . . . ?" Adelaide began.

Beatrice's shoulders were shaking. She looked up at Adelaide and Maggie, tears trickling down her cheeks into a single rivulet from her chin. The angry, frightening Beatrice was gone. Now there was only a little girl who was stuck inside a monster's stomach and badly missed her bed.

"I don't know," she cried. "Adelaide, I'm scared!"

Adelaide wanted to reach out to comfort Beatrice, but the power of Steffen's sandwiches was waning, and she found it very difficult to stand.

"Ugh . . . ," she said with a grimace. "I don't think I can make it much longer. Maggie, how are we going to get out of here? We're out of food!"

Maggie looked for the harpoon spear. But then she saw something else. It looked like a hairpin. A hairpin in the shape of a butterfly.

"I think . . . I think I found her!" she shouted. "I found Miss Delia!!"

Miss Delia lay facedown on the floor. Her hair was a knotted mess all around her head, and her hands looked cold and gray. It was too dark for Maggie to see if the librarian still breathed.

Adelaide closed her eyes and inhaled. "It has to be her! I can smell her orange hand cream!" she said. The effort made her head feel heavy again.

"Real!" Beatrice confirmed with joy.

Maggie knelt down and hoisted the frail librarian over her shoulder, almost collapsing in the process.

"We're getting weak again. How are we going to get back up to the top?" asked Adelaide.

Maggie picked up Steffen's spear and almost, just almost, felt tears rise in her eyes. "We'll use this," she said. She swung the spear over her head and threw it to the level above, where it gripped the torn floor.

The carousel shook again, and the chasm filled with what sounded like an echo of a scream. From the place where the spear pierced the floor, a black fluid oozed. The carousel's ability to repair itself was failing.

"You're going to have to hold on to each other down here," said Maggie. "The rope can't carry all three of us and Miss Delia. I'll lower the rope for you when I've gotten her out!"

"Be careful!" Adelaide told her. Maggie untied herself from the others and pulled herself up.

"Please hurry, Maggie! I'm awfully sleepy!" cried Beatrice.

Adelaide crumpled to the floor and held her head in her hands.

The sickness was strong now, and the urge to sleep was increasingly difficult to resist. She allowed her eyes to close for an instant, but the instant did not want to end.

"I can't hold my head up," she heard Beatrice say. She sounded miles away.

Adelaide's eyes fluttered open, and she saw that she was not on the carousel anymore but alone on a clipper ship. The wooden floor of the platform was a deck now, and where there had been only canopy above her, now there was a night sky full of stars and moonlight. The slow revolving had been replaced by the smooth rocking of the sea.

She rose unsteadily and held her arms out to feel the ocean spray.

"Adelaide."

The light of the moon wrapped her in its warmth. *This is where I belong,* she thought.

"Adelaide!"

She loosened her braids and let the salty breeze blow through her hair. She smiled.

"Adelaide!"

Adelaide turned around and saw Maggie standing with her.

"How did you get onto my ship?" she asked, and she felt a sadness in her heart that told her this voyage would not last.

"This isn't a ship. It's the carousel inside your head, and it's gonna be your coffin if you don't wake up," said Maggie. "Looks like I'm saving you for the fourth time, werewolf."

"No, please! Let me stay!" Adelaide pleaded.

She felt herself being shaken violently, and the ship began to blur, until it was gone. No more stars. No more ocean. Just the nightmare again.

"I got Miss Delia out. Now I'm getting you and Beatrice out of here before I'm too weak to do anything," said Maggie.

Adelaide looked up and saw that Maggie stood over her with an unconscious Beatrice draped over her shoulder.

"I don't think I can stand," said Adelaide.

Maggie yanked Adelaide up off the floor by her arm so that she stood, though she weaved sleepily from side to side. Then Maggie untied the rope from around her own waist and tied it to Adelaide's.

"If I try really hard, I can still climb the rope," said Maggie. "I'll climb to the top and pull you up. Then I'll push the two of you out while I still can."

"What about you?" asked Adelaide through half-closed eyes.

"I don't know. Maybe I can jump. Maybe I can't. Won't know until I try," said Maggie. She sounded so very distant. Up and away.

"What about Steffen?" Adelaide asked lazily.

"I couldn't find him" came Maggie's voice from the level above.

Adelaide felt herself pulled up and up, bumping against things along the way. But she was too weary to register much pain. She barely noticed when she landed on the platform above, though she did feel that something was different. The floor felt softer.

Beside her, Maggie fell down and didn't move.

"Oh dear," Beatrice mumbled feebly.

A tremendous rumbling startled each of the girls awake again.

Everything around them warped and buckled. The carousel reeled and belched, rolled and popped. Then it screeched to a stop, sending the girls sliding from one end of the floor to the other. Above them, the canopy shattered into a fine glitter, and below them, the different levels of platforms clattered together, lopsided like a pile of dirty dishes.

"What just happened?" Adelaide cried. She felt renewed energy as her heart began to pound.

"I think we hurt it . . . ," said Beatrice.

The floor buckled beneath them again and began to ooze all black and sticky. Maggie's breathing quickened as she realized just what was about to happen.

"Hold on to me!!" she rasped. They braced themselves just as a loud roar issued from the very depths of the carousel. A foamy film bled in from below. The carousel rumbled raucously, and soon it ejected the girls from the sticky platform, vomiting them onto the ground outside.

They were free, and they were not alone.

Adelaide made an effort to sit. She looked around, startled to find a battleground littered with the bodies of Widowsbury's people. Hundreds lay scattered on the dirt, soaked in white slime and the black blood of the carousel. Some were unconscious. Some moaned and groaned. Some of the more recent victims were now struggling to drag their weary bodies away from the scene, hysterical with fear. And lying not far away was Steffen. He was shivering and more than a little dazed but perfectly alive.

"Steffen!" cried Beatrice, but the reunion soon was interrupted.

Nathan Wick howled with rage and charged toward the children, his body undergoing a variety show of changes as he moved. He was tall, and he was short. He was wide, and he was thin. But no matter what, he looked nothing like the friendly Mr. Zoethout they once knew. His hands were claws, and his once-emerald eyes gleamed yellow, rimmed with red. Gone were his striped apron and straw hat, discarded as the disguises they were. Behind him, the ailing carousel—or what was left of it—creaked and groaned in pain.

Nathan bounded toward the children, tearing at his hair with every step.

"Why are you trying to stop me?" he demanded. "These people hate you! They want you to suffer! Let them die!"

"And to think I used to believe you were a friend!" said Steffen, disappointed.

Nathan threw back his head and laughed a madman's laugh.

"Your friend? Your friend, little Widowsburian? I was never your friend!" he spat. "I have hated you and your *friends* from the very beginning, your awful memories filling my head. Making me doubt myself. The others were easy to manipulate, but not you four! Why, I even pitied you! I almost reconsidered everything on account of that pity! I had to wait for you to come to *me* to destroy you, and even now you've gotten in my way. We have the very same enemies. You should be glad to sacrifice yourselves just to be rid of them all!"

"How could anything these people did have made you so evil?" Adelaide asked feebly.

Nathan stared at her in astonishment.

"How can you ask me that?" he said. Fresh tears ran down his bony cheeks. "You saw my memories. They aren't so very different from your own! Are you so blinded by everything they've told you that you really can't see the answer? Yes! Yes, they must die! And it should have happened by now. Here, in the very hour that Margret Bellhouse died so long ago."

He pulled out his pocket watch and admired it sadly before closing his hand around it. "But punctuality is not as important as completion. We will continue as planned," he said. "And after Widowsbury is destroyed, we'll travel onward. We will not stop until every wretched person on this earth has been swallowed up forever."

"Why? Why the whole world?" asked Maggie.

"Because only then will we be left alone. Only when they are dead will the world stop hurting us," Nathan answered. "When they are all gone, we shall fade away together. We are part of each other, the creature and I. I cannot live without it, and it cannot live without me. But we will die knowing we have triumphed!"

"That won't fix anything!" said Steffen. "How can anyone treat you better if you've killed them all?"

Nathan groaned, and his stretched-out figure shrank to something like a normal man's. He looked withered, and his yellow eyes had lost some of their glow against his graying skin. He reached a hand down and ruffled Steffen's hair, and he did not seem to notice that Steffen shuddered. He surveyed the scene with all the townspeople lying there, crying and moaning and calling out for loved ones. Then he turned to the four children and extended his bone-thin hand.

"I don't have to kill them all," he said.

They stared at him.

"You could join me," he continued. "You're like me. Don't you see? I have hated you for that, but I realize now that you could be my companions. We need each other, I think."

"And you wouldn't try to kill us again?" asked Beatrice.

Nathan chuckled and shook his head. "I can overreact at times," he said. "For that I am deeply sorry. We've been abandoned by our parents. Unloved by our peers. Tortured by a community that swore to look out for its own! Why should we not benefit from brotherhood as well?"

He knelt down and traced Beatrice's cheek with a long, sharp nail.

"You would like to be free, wouldn't you?" he said to her.

"Beatrice, get away from him . . . ," said Maggie, but she was far too weak to get up.

Beatrice smiled strangely. "Would you take care of us?" she asked Nathan.

"We would take care of each other," Nathan answered, and he tapped her nose.

"I would like that," said Beatrice. She did not sound herself.

Adelaide, too, thought about Nathan's suggestion. Traveling the world with only your friends and a creature that eats everyone you don't like; it was the sort of fantasy she'd had when she was small.

But that was just the problem. It was a child's fantasy, and she was growing up! Nathan Wick was nothing more than an angry child in a man-monster's body.

And how dare he say that about their parents? How dare he say that about everyone else in the world when there were kind people in it like Miss Delia? To think he was trying to convert Beatrice, who only ever saw the best in everyone. That was unforgivable.

Adelaide managed to stand despite her wobbling legs.

"Leave Beatrice alone," she growled. She mustered all her dwindling strength and lunged at him, but with no effort at all, he knocked her aside.

Beatrice blinked, confused. A few feet away, Adelaide fought for breath and spoke despite the pain in her side.

"I'd rather stay in Widowsbury with these people than be with you!" she rasped.

Nathan glared at her. "What?" he said through his teeth. His fingers, once outstretched in invitation, curled into a fist.

"We'll never be like you," Adelaide continued. "People are cruel when they don't understand you. That's just how they are. You think we can't be cruel, too? Look at what you've done! Margret didn't kill your family. She didn't burn down your house. She just broke your heart, and you're the one who turned into a monster! I don't want to be a part of that!"

"*We* don't want to be a part of that!" Steffen added weakly. He let his head rest in the mud again.

Nathan withdrew his hand and glared at each of the children.

Maggie guarding the ailing Steffen. Little Beatrice, shaking the fog from her head. Adelaide hugging her bruised ribs.

"You . . . ," he spat. "You've betrayed me! You're just like them!"

The earth began to tremble.

"You were supposed to understand me!" he cried out.

He stumbled backward onto the crumbled heap of his carousel, his only friend. His conspirator. The extension of all his blackest feelings. He crawled along the tilted platform and sobbed into the planks. Inside him, the loathing and heartache seethed. It dribbled out of his mouth in a blackish foam. The children could only watch in horror.

And then, strangely, the carousel began to turn. With one final burst of energy, it carried Nathan as it had once carried them and increased to an insane whirl, lopsided and sick. Stranger still, Nathan's skin started to bubble and pop. The carousel, too, warped and melted along with him. He did nothing to stop it. At last, he let out a howl of anguish and raised his claw-hands to the sky, spitting curses at the cloud-covered moon. The curses had barely left his melting lips when the carousel and he dissolved into nothing but a sticky black pool, draining into the cracks of the earth.

All that was left of Nathan Wick and his creature was a pocket watch made of bone with hands made of beetle legs.

"He's gone," said Adelaide.

"Thank goodness," Maggie muttered.

"Poor, poor, Nathan Wick," Beatrice cried.

Steffen was too overcome by exhaustion to say much of

anything. Succumbing to his weariness at last, he curled up in the dirt and closed his eyes. The others couldn't help doing the same. Just before sleep overtook Adelaide, she heard someone whisper and felt a brush of ice against her ear.

"Thank you, Adelaide Foss," said a voice she knew was Margret Bellhouse's. Then the breath on her ear was nothing again, and Adelaide dreamed peacefully of sailing ships on cloudless summer nights.

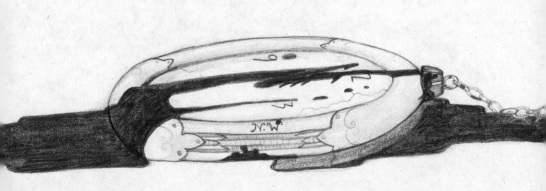

- CHAPTER TWELVE -
Skary Childrin

I t was a humble victory.

There would be no celebration. No parades. No medals of honor for the four heroes who had saved a town and quite possibly the world. For their troubles, Adelaide, Beatrice, Maggie, and Steffen received only a brief hospital stay, punctuated by jabs from syringes and sips of pea-potato puree through a straw. What else could be expected from a place so used to bad luck, whose pride was as bruised as its arms and legs? Did anyone even know who had saved them?

Not that the children expected anything more. A simple "thanks" would've been nice, but that was going to be a long while. By then, anybody who knew the truth would have forgotten them.

For now, no one called them mean names, and that was reward enough. Even Becky Buschard kept to herself, though she still glared menacingly at Adelaide whenever she could. Adelaide didn't mind that as much now. How it must have burned Becky to owe her life to the girls she hated most! The thought made Adelaide smile. Indeed, revenge was sweet.

But no sooner had they returned to school than Adelaide, Beatrice, and Maggie found themselves called to Mrs. Merryweather's office.

"She can't possibly be giving us detention already," said Beatrice as they waited outside the headmistress's doors.

"Business as usual. I'm sure we broke some rules," Maggie retorted.

"She's certainly not giving us any awards," said Adelaide.

The doors opened, and Mrs. Merryweather's secretary appeared. She looked exceptionally wan. But then so did most of the town.

"Mrs. Merryweather will see you now," she said, and she held open the door. This was most unusual. Normally, she let it slam in their faces.

"Come in, ladies," said Mrs. Merryweather from her inner office. She sounded weary.

The girls took their seats in the three uncomfortable wooden chairs before the headmistress's desk. These were the chairs in which they'd each been interrogated time after time. Usually for things they hadn't done, but occasionally for things they had. Just the feel of the varnished mahogany made their palms sweat.

"You may relax," said Mrs. Merryweather, "but I will expect to see straight backs and feet flat on the floor for the rest of the day. Do you understand me?"

The girls nodded, but being told to relax and actually being able to do so were ideas miles apart.

Mrs. Merryweather stared down at her desk. She seemed powerless. Adelaide wondered whether this was the result of the carousel or if she simply saw the headmistress differently now.

"I will keep this brief, as you have each been away from your classes, and the holidays are upon us. I've no doubt you have much catch-up work to do," she said, but still she could not look them in the eye.

"I have decided," she continued slowly, for it must have pained her to say it, "that you may join the others at recess from this day forward."

"You mean outside?" said Adelaide.

"Not on the Wall?" asked Beatrice.

"Huh?" said Maggie.

"Yes," Mrs. Merryweather replied tersely, "and you may participate in field trips. That is, when we're able to have them again. But I am warning you . . ."

Adelaide considered that she might be dreaming all of this, but she noticed with a clarity not normally attributed to dreams that Mrs. Merryweather's warning voice sounded less severe than it had before.

"Do not make me regret granting this privilege," Mrs. Merryweather said, staring each of them directly in the eyes for the first time since they'd come into her office.

"Yes, Mrs. Merryweather," they answered at once. The headmistress's glare wavered, and she quickly looked down at the piles of paperwork before her.

"Thank you, girls. That will be all. Go on to breakfast. Miss Peet will be delivering the Lecture today as I have far too many business matters to address before our winter break," she said, and she waved them away.

They left her office, bewildered and unsure if they should be happy or afraid.

"Outside? Field trips?" Beatrice whispered as they walked down the hall.

"Miss Peet?" said Adelaide. "Surely, she doesn't mean . . ."

It was then that they crossed paths with someone they had once been certain they would never, ever see again. She had neat little round glasses and auburn hair in a bun. Fastened to it was a pin in the shape of a monarch butterfly.

"Miss Delia!" Beatrice squeaked. She ran and threw her arms around the librarian with such force the woman all but lost her balance.

"Oof!" said Miss Delia.

Adelaide hugged her next. This move dislodged her braids from the tops of her pointed ears, but for once, she did not care.

Maggie gave the librarian a little wave and stuck her hands back in her pockets.

"Hey," she said.

"Hello, ladies," Miss Delia said warmly.

"We didn't know if you'd made it or not!" said Beatrice. "You don't know how much trouble we got into just trying to find you!"

"We went to the Wailing Room and everything!" said Adelaide, who then, remembering her pride, dislodged herself from the librarian and coughed.

"Beatrice, dear, you're going to cut off the circulation to my legs," said Miss Delia.

Beatrice apologized and released the librarian from her grasp.

"And find me you did," said Miss Delia. "Rumor has it that you three are responsible for a great deal more than that. Quite the heroes you are."

"We're glad you're back, Miss Delia," said Adelaide, "but now we don't have detention anymore. I'm not sure what I think about that."

Miss Delia was perplexed. "But aren't you pleased?" she asked. "No more sentences! Sunshine! Er, at least . . . the outdoors, I mean."

"Yeah. Sure. It's *great*," Maggie snorted.

"What I think Maggie and Adelaide are saying is . . ." Beatrice hesitated. "We've sort of . . . forgotten how to play with the others."

"They're going to make fun of us," said Adelaide. "Things are all right now, but it'll only be a matter of time before it's just like the old days."

Miss Delia put her hands on her hips. "Are you really so afraid of a little ridicule?" she laughed. "After everything you've faced?"

"You don't know how awful they can be!" said Adelaide.

"I know it better than you might think," said Miss Delia. "I also know—and so do they, deep down—how fantastic you can be. So, you go out there for recess today, tomorrow, and every day after. If they give you trouble, just remember how much more you accomplished in only the past week than they can ever hope to."

"But," said Beatrice, "can we still come and see you?"

"Of course you can!" said Miss Delia. "In fact, you must promise me you will! Mrs. Merryweather has given me permission to remodel the library, you see, and it's going to be absolutely wonderful! New paint, new furniture, new books, and so many delightful things to do. Oh, you'll have such fun when it's finished! Even you, Maggie!"

"So, you'll stay? You're not scared of this place?" asked Maggie.

"Pish tosh," said Miss Delia. "Bad things happen everywhere in the world, not just in Widowsbury. If we run away every time we have a nightmare, we'll never really wake up. There's so much to like about this town, once you get used to it. No sunburns! No droughts! And you all do such interesting things with silk flowers! I never thought of doing a whole garden that way."

She gathered up her papers and books and tucked in the loose pages.

"Besides," she added, "how often could something as terrible as *that* happen in the same place?"

"Actually—" Adelaide began, but she was interrupted by the bell for Breakfast Time, and Miss Delia hurried down to the dining hall.

"Oh dear," said Beatrice.

"She's still got a lot to learn about Widowsbury, hasn't she?" said Maggie.

First Class. Homemaking Sciences. Adelaide poured some tea in the sugar dish before she caught herself. But Mrs. Hazel admitted the dishes were similar and allowed her to try again. She finally got it right and passed her Graceful Serving exam.

Second Class. Ladies' Literature. Nobody glued Adelaide's book together, and she even found the courage to raise her hand to read aloud. She wasn't chosen until the end, but she *was* chosen.

Third Class. Mathematics. She thought Shelley Aires was going to ask to copy her answers, but the note Shelley passed this time was different. "Sorry" was all it said, which Adelaide took to mean, *I'm sorry for copying and getting you in trouble last week.* Or close enough. "It's okay," Adelaide wrote back. And it was.

On the way to lunch, Adelaide passed by the gardener and the janitor. She couldn't be sure, but out of the corner of her eye, it looked like they nodded to her.

"Everybody's acting so strange around us today," said Adelaide at lunchtime. "It's like they're not really being nice. They're just . . ."

"Not being mean," Beatrice finished.

"Yeah," said Maggie. "It's weird."

Adelaide pointed to Beatrice's pocket. "What's Phillip got to say about all this?" she asked. But Beatrice just shrugged.

"He finally decided it was time to play with the other ghost mice, and I agreed. You can't go around hiding in people's pockets forever," she said.

"Are you all right with that? He was your best friend," said Adelaide.

"I'll miss him, but it's better this way," said Beatrice. "Besides, I have people friends now! Living ones!"

Her face fell. "I feel so awful for poor Nathan Wick, though," she said. "He never got to have any friends. Do you suppose that's why he didn't try harder to save himself? Because he was alone? Like we used to be?"

Neither Maggie nor Adelaide had an answer to that question. It made them uncomfortable just thinking about it. *We could've been just like him one day,* thought Adelaide. *We could've given in when he wanted us to, and none of these other people would be here today.*

She could still see Nathan's face as he died. So much sorrow. So much hurt. In some ways, no matter how evil the man was, Adelaide would always feel that she had betrayed the only other person who understood them. But she reminded herself that Nathan Wick betrayed them, too, and would never have stopped until the end.

The recess bell rang, creating a welcome distraction. No more of that disturbing talk. Now was the time for them to go out and be normal children. If they could just sort out what that entailed.

Outside, the Widowsbury sky looked just as gray as it had for the past twelve years. The wind, it seemed, was calmer today, but it was neither warmer nor any colder. Life for the little town in the valley, curses and all, would go on just as before. After the wild past few days, however, Adelaide had to admit she didn't mind it so much.

"Adelaide! Beatrice! Maggie! Hey!" someone yelled just beyond the chain-link fence.

"Steffen!" Beatrice cheered.

Steffen jogged over from across the street and waved enthusiastically. He was wearing new glasses and, for once, he didn't carry a knapsack.

"Guess what!" he said, his whole face a smile. "I've been made an honorary Rudyard Boy! They're going to let me go to school next year and everything, and my dad doesn't have to pay for it! Boy, was he surprised when we got called into Mr. Edwin's office today! I'll even have a uniform!"

"That's wonderful, Steffen!" said Beatrice.

"No it's not. It's a monkey suit. But whatever. Congratulations, Steffen," said Maggie grouchily. Then she laughed and reached over the fence to knock Steffen's cap off his head.

"Don't pay any attention to Maggie. I'm just glad you're happy, Steffen," said Adelaide, though she felt a little sad. She didn't like to think of Steffen sitting still in a classroom with a pencil instead of outdoors, working on some strange invention. But she reminded herself that this was what her friend wanted, and it didn't have to mean his personality would change, or that he'd try to fill the snooty shoes of Henry Fernberger, who she had heard was now being tutored at home.

"Oh, I almost forgot!" said Steffen. "My dad's giving me his old typewriter for Christmas. It was supposed to be a surprise, but I sort of found it already. Anyway, I'm going to use it to write a story about us and send it to the adventure magazines. I think I'm going to call it 'Steffen and Adelaide and Maggie and Beatrice Versus the Carousel.'"

"Bit long, don't you think?" said Maggie.

"I don't know. I'm not so good at making up names for things," Steffen admitted.

"What if we came up with a name for ourselves? Then you

wouldn't have to name each one of us in the title," Adelaide suggested.

Beatrice clapped. "Oh, I like that!" she said. "What would it be? What about Three Girls and a Boy?"

Steffen and Maggie made faces. "I guess it's accurate, but . . . ," said Adelaide.

"All right. Fine. You three are the creative ones. I'll take notes," said Beatrice. She pulled a folded spelling paper from her pocket along with a fat black crayon, and the meeting commenced.

Steffen suggested The Amazing Four. Maggie said The Kids should suffice. Less was more, after all. But neither of those really sounded right. Then Adelaide remembered a little song. It went to the tune of "Frère Jacques," and it used to make her so angry! But now it was perfect, and it was *them*.

"The Scary Children," she said.

Beatrice giggled.

"I think I like it," said Maggie, but Steffen was confused.

"I don't really get it. How are we supposed to be heroes if we're scary?" he asked.

"Because that's what people think we are, and I'm not ashamed of it anymore," said Adelaide.

"Neither'm I!" said Beatrice as she scribbled on the back of her paper.

"Well . . . okay," said Steffen. "I do think it's a little odd. But then, I guess, so are we."

"The Scary Children it is!" Beatrice chirped. She slashed a few dramatic lines across the paper and then held it up for all to see.

THE SKARY CHILDRIN vs THE CAROSELL

it said in thick black lines, and at the end of a series of dashed loops, she had drawn a butterfly in flight.

"Beatrice, I hate to break it to you, but your spelling . . . ," Maggie began. Then she thought better of it with the help of a pointed glare from Adelaide. ". . . is just fine. Couldn't have written it better myself."